Dear Reader,

The inimitable Audrey Hepburn famously said she liked fairy tales best of all and, finally, I have something in common with her!

I, too, love fairy tales. I think they've endured and entertained for a very particular reason—wrapped up in the magical creatures and crowns are emotional experiences and truths that resonate within everyone.

For me *The Ugly Duckling* is particularly relatable. Who hasn't ever felt awkward or as if they don't belong? And many of us have experienced loneliness or bullying.

So it's wonderfully moving to journey with a character who's survived hardships and see them grow into the person they're meant to be. And it's the hurt on the inside that is far harder to overcome than an external makeover—fun as that is!

Hester is my "ugly duckling." I loved gifting her Alek, who holds up the mirror, enabling her to see her beauty—both internal and external—and believe in who she really is. It's that self-belief that then allows her to accept love.

I hope you enjoy Hester's transformation and her impact on Alek in turn...in his discovery of the magic of love.

Sincerely,

Natalie

Once Upon a Temptation

Will they live passionately ever after?

Once upon a time, in a land far, far away, there was a billionaire—or eight! Each billionaire had riches beyond your wildest imagination. Still, they were each missing something: love. But the path to true love is never easy...even if you're one of the world's richest men!

Inspired by fairy tales like *Beauty and the Beast* and *Little Red Riding Hood*, the Once Upon a Temptation collection will take you on a passion-filled journey of ultimate escapism.

Fall in love with...

Cinderella's Royal Secret by Lynne Graham

Beauty and Her One-Night Baby by Dani Collins

Shy Queen in the Royal Spotlight
by Natalie Anderson

Claimed in the Italian's Castle by Caitlin Crews

Expecting His Billion-Dollar Scandal
by Cathy Williams

Taming the Big Bad Billionaire by Pippa Roscoe

The Flaw in His Marriage Plan by Tara Pammi

His Innocent's Passionate Awakening
by Melanie Milburne

Natalie Anderson

———

SHY QUEEN IN THE ROYAL SPOTLIGHT

HARLEQUIN®
PRESENTS®

Recycling programs
for this product may
not exist in your area.

ISBN-13: 978-1-335-89374-1

Shy Queen in the Royal Spotlight

Copyright © 2020 by Natalie Anderson

This edition published by arrangement with Harlequin Books S.A.

For questions and comments about the quality of this book,
please contact us at CustomerService@Harlequin.com.

Harlequin Enterprises ULC
22 Adelaide St. West, 40th Floor
Toronto, Ontario M5H 4E3, Canada
www.Harlequin.com

Printed in U.S.A.

USA TODAY bestselling author **Natalie Anderson** writes emotional contemporary romance full of sparkling banter, sizzling heat and uplifting endings—perfect for readers who love to escape with empowered heroines and arrogant alphas who are too sexy for their own good.

When she's not writing, you'll find Natalie wrangling her four children, three cats, two goldfish and one dog...and snuggled in a heap on the sofa with her husband at the end of the day. Follow her at natalie-anderson.com.

Books by Natalie Anderson

Harlequin Presents

The Forgotten Gallo Bride
Claiming His Convenient Fiancée
The King's Captive Virgin
Awakening His Innocent Cinderella
Pregnant by the Commanding Greek
The Greek's One-Night Heir

Conveniently Wed!

The Innocent's Emergency Wedding

One Night With Consequences

Princess's Pregnancy Secret

The Throne of San Felipe

The Secret That Shocked De Santis
The Mistress That Tamed De Santis

Visit the Author Profile page
at Harlequin.com for more titles.

For my own Prince Charming and the four delightful sprites we've been blessed with.

I love you.

CHAPTER ONE

'Fɪ?'

Hester Moss heard the front door slam and froze.

'Fifi? Damn it, where the hell are you?'

Fifi?

Hester gaped as it dawned on her just who the owner of that voice was. As Princess Fiorella's assistant while she was studying in Boston, Hester had met a few of the important people the Princess consorted with, but she'd been in the Princess's *brother's* presence only once. That one time there'd been many present and she certainly hadn't spoken to him. But, like everyone, she knew he was outrageous, arrogant and entitled. Not surprising given he ruled the stunning Mediterranean island kingdom that was the world's favourite playground.

She'd had no idea he was coming to visit his sister. It wasn't in the immaculate schedule she kept for the Princess, nor in any correspondence. Surely it would have been all in caps, bold, underlined *and* highlighted if it had been planned? Perhaps he was trying to fly beneath the radar—after all, he attracted huge publicity wherever he went. But if that were the case, why was he *shouting*?

'Fifi?'

No one spoke with such familiarity to the Princess, or with such audible impatience. For a split second Hester considered staying silent and hiding, but she suspected it was only a matter of seconds before he stormed into her bedroom. With a cautious glance at the corner Hester sped to the door and quickly stepped out into their living room.

And there he was. Prince Alek Salustri of Triscari, currently turning the lounge she and the Princess shared into a Lilliputian-sized container—one that was far too small to hold a man like him. Not just a prince. Not just powerful. He was lithe, honed perfection and for a moment all Hester could do was stare—inhaling the way his jet-black suit covered his lean muscled frame. The black shirt beneath the superbly tailored jacket was teamed with a sleek, matte-black tie and he held his dark-lensed aviator sunglasses in his hand, totally exuding impatience and danger. It was more than the bespoke clothing and luxurious style. He was so at ease in his place in the world—monstrously self-assured and confident because he just owned it. Everything. Except right now?

He was angry. The moment his coal-black gaze landed on her, he grew angrier still.

'Oh.' His frown slipped from surly all the way down to thunderous. 'You're the secretary.'

Not for the first time Hester found herself in the position of not being who or what had been hoped for. But she was too practised at masking emotion to flinch. No matter what, she never let anyone see they'd struck a nerve. And being the source of irritation for a spoilt playboy prince? Didn't bother her in the least.

'Your Highness.' She nodded, but her knees had locked too tight to perform a curtsey. 'Unfortunately Princess Fiorella isn't here.'

'I can see that.' He ground his teeth. 'Where is she?'

She kept her hands at her sides, refusing to curl them into fists and reveal any anxiety. It was her job to protect Princess Fiorella from unwanted interruption, only Prince Alek wasn't just higher up the ladder than most of the people she shielded the Princess from, he was at the very top. The apex predator himself.

'At a bio lab,' Hester drew breath and answered. 'She should be back in about half an hour unless she decides to go for a coffee instead of coming back here right away.'

'Damn.' Another stormy emotion flashed across his face and he turned to pace across the room. 'She's with people?'

Hester nodded.

'And no phone?'

'Her bodyguard has one but the Princess prefers to be able to concentrate in class without interruption. Would you like me to message—?'

'No,' he snapped. 'I need to see her alone. I'll wait for her here.'

He still looked so fierce that Hester was tempted to send a quick message regardless. Except blatantly disobeying his order didn't seem wise.

She watched warily as he paced, brusquely sidestepping Hester's scrupulously clean desk.

'Is there anything I can help you with?' She was annoyed with how nervous her query sounded. She was never nervous dealing with Princess Fiorella. But she wasn't quite sure how to handle this man. Any man, actually.

He paused and regarded her, seeming to see her properly for the first time. She stared back, acutely aware of his coal-black bottomless gaze. Whether those beautiful eyes were soulful or soul*less*, she wasn't sure. She only knew she couldn't tear her own away.

With slow-dawning horror she realised the inanity of her question. As if she could ever help him? He was Prince Alek—the Prince of Night, of Sin…of *Scandal*.

His phone buzzed and he answered it impatiently. 'I've already said no,' he snapped after a moment.

Even from across the room Hester heard the pleading tones of someone remonstrating.

'I will not do that,' the Prince said firmly. 'I've already stated there will be no damn marriage. I have no desire to—' He broke off and looked grim as he listened. 'Then we will find another way. I will not—' He broke off again with a smothered curse and then launched into a volley of Italian.

Hester stared at the top of her desk and wished she could disappear. Clearly he wasn't concerned enough by her presence to bother remaining polite or care that she could hear him berating the ancient laws of his own lands.

The world had been waiting for him to be crowned since his father's death ten months ago, but he hadn't because 'Playboy Prince Alek' had so far shown little interest in acquiring the wife necessary for his coronation to occur. None of those billion *Ten Best Possible Brides* lists scattered across the world's media had apparently inspired him. Nor had the growing impatience of his people.

Perhaps he'd been taking time to get over his

father's passing. Hester had seen Princess Fiorella's bereft grief and had tried to alleviate any stresses on the younger woman as best she could because she knew how devastating and how incredibly isolating it was to become an orphan. She'd been pleased to see the Princess had begun spending more time with friends recently. But Prince Alek hadn't retreated from his social life—in fact he'd accelerated it. In the last month he'd been photographed with a different woman every other night as if he were flaunting his refusal to do as that old law decreed and settle down.

Now the Prince growled and shoved his phone back into his pocket, turning to face her. As she desperately tried to think of something innocuous to say a muffled thud echoed from the bedroom she'd stepped out of. Hester maintained her dispassionate expression but it was too much to hope he hadn't heard it.

'What was that?' He cocked his head, looking just like that predator whose acute hearing had picked up the unmistakable sounds of nearby prey. 'Why won't you let me into her room?'

'Nothing—'

'I'm her *brother*. What are you hiding? Is she in there with a man or something?'

Before she could move, the Prince strode past her and opened the door as if he owned the place.

'Of course you would think that,' she muttered crossly, running after him.

He'd halted just inside the doorway. 'What the hell is that?'

'A terrified cat, no thanks to you.' She pushed past him and carefully crept forward so as not to frighten the hissing half-wild thing any more than it already was.

'What's it doing in here?'

'Having dinner.' She gingerly picked it up and opened the window. 'Or at least, it was.'

'I can't believe Fi owns that cat.' He stared at the creature with curling cynicism. 'Not exactly a thoroughbred Prussian Blue, is she?'

Hester's anger smoked. Of course he wouldn't see past the exterior of the grey and greyer, mangled-eared, all but feral cat. '*He* might not be handsome, but he's lonely and vulnerable. He eats in here every day.' She set him down on the narrow ledge.

'How on earth does he get down?' He walked to the window and watched beside her as the cat carefully climbed down to the last available fire escape rung before practically flying the last ten feet to the ground. 'Impressive.'

'He knows how to survive.' But as Hester glared at the Prince her nose tingled. She blinked rapidly but couldn't hold back her usual reaction.

'Did you just sneeze?' Prince Alek turned that

unfathomable stare on her. 'Are you *allergic* to cats?'

'Well, why should he starve just because I'm a bad fit for him?' She plucked a tissue from the packet on the bedside table and blew her nose pointedly.

But apparently the Prince had lost interest already, because he was now studying the narrow bedroom with a scowl.

'I'd no idea Fi read so many thrillers.' He picked up the tome next to the tissues. 'I thought she was all animals. And how does she even move in this space?'

Hester awkwardly watched, trying to see the room through his eyes. A narrow white box with a narrow white bed. A neat pile of books. An occasional cat. A complete cliché.

'Where's she put all her stuff?' He frowned, running a finger over the small wooden box that was the only decorative item in the room.

Hester stilled and faced the wretched moment. 'This isn't Princess Fiorella's bedroom.' She gritted her teeth for a second and then continued. 'It's mine.'

He froze then shot her a look of fury and chagrin combined, snatching his finger from tracing the carved grooves in the lid of the box. 'Why didn't you say so sooner?'

'You stormed in here before I had the chance.

I guess you're used to doing anything you want,' she snapped, embarrassed by the invasion of privacy and her own failure to speak up sooner.

But then she realised what she'd said and she couldn't suck it back. She clasped her hands in front of her but kept her head high and her features calm.

Never show them you're afraid.

She'd learned long ago how to act around people with power over her, how to behave in the hope bullies would get bored and leave her alone. With stillness and calm—on the outside at least.

Prince Alek stared at her for a long moment in stunned silence. But then his expression transformed, a low rumble of laughter sounded and suddenly Hester was the one stunned.

Dimples. On a grown man. And they were gorgeous.

Her jaw dropped as his mood flipped from frustrated to good-humoured in a lightning flash.

'You think I'm spoilt?' he asked as his laughter ebbed.

'Aren't you?' she answered before thinking.

His smile was everything. A wide slash across that perfect face that somehow elevated it beyond angelically beautiful, to warm and human. Even with those perfectly straight white teeth he looked roguish. That twist of his full lips was a touch lopsided and the cute creases in his cheeks appearing and disappearing like a playful cupid's wink.

'I wouldn't think that being forced to find a bride is in the definition of being spoiled,' he said lazily.

'You mean for your coronation?' She could hardly pretend not to know about it when she'd overheard half that phone call.

'Yes. My coronation,' he echoed dryly, leaving her room with that leisurely, relaxed manner that belied the speed and strength of him. 'They won't change that stupid law.'

'Are you finding the democratic process a bitter pill to swallow?' she asked, oddly pleased that the man didn't get everything his own way. 'Won't all the old boys do what you want them to?'

He turned to stare at her coolly, the dimples dispelled, but she gazed back limpidly.

'It's an archaic law,' he said quietly. 'It ought to have been changed years ago.'

'It's tradition,' she replied, walking past him into the centre of the too-small living room. 'Perhaps there's something appealing about stability.'

'Stability?'

There was something impish in his echo that caused her to swiftly glance back. She caught him eyeing her rear end. A startling wave of heat rose within—exasperating her. She knew he wasn't interested, he was just so highly sexed he couldn't help himself assessing any passing woman. Her just-smoking anger sizzled.

'Of having a monarch who's not distracted and chasing skirt all the time,' she said pointedly.

His lips curled. 'Not *all* the time. I like to rest on Thursdays.' He leaned against the doorframe to her bedroom.

'So it's a rest day today?'

'Of course.' His gaze glanced down her body in a swift assessment but then returned to her face and all trace of humour was gone. 'Do you truly think it's okay to force someone to get *married* before they can do the job they've spent their life training for?'

There was a throb of tension despite the light way he asked the question. He cocked his head, daring her to answer honestly. 'You think I should sacrifice my personal life for my country?'

Actually she thought nothing of the sort but she'd backed herself into a corner by arguing with him. 'I think there could be benefits in an arranged union.'

'Benefits?' His eyebrows lifted, scepticism oozing from his perfect pores. 'What possible benefits could there be?'

Oh, he really didn't want his continuous smorgasbord of women curtailed in any way, did he?

'What if you have the right contract with the

right bride?' she argued emotionlessly. 'You both know what you're heading into. It's a cool, logical decision for the betterment of your nation.'

'Cool and logical?' His eyebrows arched. 'What are you, an android?'

Right now, she rather wished she were. It was maddening that she found him attractive—especially when she knew what a player he was. Doubtless this was how every woman who came within a hundred feet of him felt, which was exactly why he was able to play as hard and as frequently as he did. When a man was that blessed by the good-looks gods, mere mortals like her had little defence against him.

'Perhaps when you're King you can lobby for the change.' She shrugged, wanting to close the conversation she never should have started.

'Indeed. But apparently in order to become King I must marry.'

'It's quite the conundrum for you,' she said lightly.

'It has no bearing on my ability to do my job. It's an anachronism.'

'Then why not just make an arrangement with one of your many "friends"?' she muttered with frustration. 'I'm sure they'd all be willing to bear the burden of being your bride.'

He laughed and a gleam flickered in his eyes. 'Don't think I haven't thought about it. Problem is they'd all take it too seriously and assume it was going to be happily ever after.'

'Yes, I imagine that would be a problem.' She nodded, primly sarcastic.

He straightened from the doorway and stepped closer. 'Not for someone like you, though.'

'Pardon?'

'You'd understand the arrangement perfectly well and I get the impression the last thing you'd want is happily ever after with me.'

Too stunned—and somehow hurt—to stop, she answered back sharply. 'I just don't imagine it would be possible.'

Those eyebrows arched again. 'With anyone or only with me?'

She suddenly remembered who it was she'd just insulted. 'Sorry.' She clamped her lips together.

'Don't be, you're quite right,' he said with another low laugh. 'The difficulty I have is finding someone who understands the situation, its limitations, and who has the discretion to pull it off.'

'Quite a tall order.' She wished he'd leave. Or let her leave. Because somehow this was dangerous. *He* was dangerous.

He eyed her for another long moment before glancing to survey the neat desk she'd retreated behind. 'You're the epitome of discretion.'

'Because my desk is tidy?'

'Because you're smart enough to understand such an arrangement.' He lifted his chin and arrogantly speared her with his mesmerising gaze. 'And we have no romantic history to get tangled in,' he drawled. 'In fact, I think you might be my perfect bride.'

There was a look on his face—a mischievous delight tempting her to smile and join the joke. But this wasn't funny.

So she sent him a dismissive glance before turning to stare at her desk. 'No.'

'Why not?' The humour dropped from his voice and left only cool calculation.

Definitely dangerous. Definitely more ruthless than his careless façade suggested.

'You're not serious,' she said.

'Actually, I rather think I am.'

'No,' she repeated, but her voice faded. She forced her arms across her waist to stop herself moving restlessly, to stop that insidious heat from rising, to stop temptation escaping her control.

She *never* felt temptation. She never *felt*. She'd been too busy trying to simply survive for so long…but now?

His gaze didn't leave her face. 'Why not take a moment to think about it?'

'What is there to think about?' she asked with exaggerated disbelief. 'It's preposterous.'

And it was. He'd walked in less than five minutes ago and was now proposing. He was certifiable.

'I don't think so,' he countered calmly. 'I think it could work very well.'

He made it seem easy, as if it were nothing.

'You don't think you should take this a little more seriously instead of proposing to the first woman you see today?'

'Why shouldn't I propose to you?'

Hester breathed slowly, struggling to slow her building anger. 'No one would ever believe you'd want to marry me.'

'Why?'

She mentally begged for mercy. 'Because I'm nothing like the women you normally date.'

His gaze skidded down her in that cool and yet hot assessing way again. 'I disagree.'

She gritted her teeth. She didn't need him to start telling her she was attractive in a false show of charm.

'It's just clothes and make-up.' He stole the wind from her sails. 'Fancy packaging.'

'Smoke and mirrors?' She swallowed the bitterness that rose within her because she just knew how little the world thought of her 'packaging'. 'I meant I'm not from your level of society. I'm not a *princess*.'

'So? These "levels" shouldn't matter.' He shrugged carelessly.

'I'm not even from your country,' she continued, ignoring his interruption. 'It's not what's expected of you.'

He glanced beyond her, seeming to study some speck on the wall behind her. 'I'll do as they dictate, but they don't get to dictate *everything*. I don't want to marry anyone, certainly not a princess. I'll choose who I want.' His gaze flicked back to her, that arrogant amusement gleaming again. 'It would be quite the fairy tale.'

'It would be quite unbelievable,' she countered acerbically. She couldn't believe he was even continuing this conversation.

'Why would it, though?' he pondered. 'You've been working for Fi for how long?'

'Twelve months.'

'But you knew her before that.'

'For three months before, yes.'

Hester had been assigned as Princess Fiorella's roommate when the Princess came to America to study. Hester was four years older and already into her graduate studies so it had been more of a study support role. It turned out that Fiorella was smart as, and hadn't needed much tutoring, but it hadn't been long before Hester had begun helping her with her mountains of correspondence, to the point that Fiorella had asked her to work for her on a formal basis. It had enabled Hester to reduce her other varsity tutoring, she'd finished her thesis and now focused on her voluntary work at the drop-in centre in the city.

She scheduled Fiorella's diaries, replied to messages and emails and organised almost everything without leaving their on-campus apartment. It was perfect.

'Then you've passed all our security checks and proven your ability to meet our family's specific demands.' Prince Alek took another step closer towards her.

Hester stared at him, unable to believe he was still going with this.

'Furthermore it's perfectly believable that we would know each other behind palace walls,' he added. 'No one knows what might have been going on within the privacy of the palace.'

'Sorry to poke holes in your narrative, but I've never actually *been* to the palace,' she pointed out tartly. She'd never been to Triscari. In fact, she'd never been out of the country at all. 'In addition, we've been in the same airspace only once before.'

Prince Alek had escorted Fiorella to the university in lieu of the King all those months ago.

'And this is the first time we've actually spoken,' she finished, proving the impossibility of his proposal with a tilt of her chin.

'I'm flattered you've kept count.' His wolfish smile flashed. 'No one else needs know that though. For all anyone else knows, the times I've called or visited Fi might've been a cover to see you.' He nodded slowly and that thoughtful look deepened as he stepped closer still. 'It could work very well.'

Hester's low-burning anger lifted. How could he assume this would work so easily? Did he think she'd be instantly compliant? Or flattered even? He really was a prince—used to people bowing and scraping and catering to his every whim. Had he ever been told no? If not, his response was going to be interesting.

'Well, thank you all the same, Your Highness.' She cleared her throat. 'But my answer is no. Why don't I tell your sister you'll be waiting for her at your usual hotel?'

She wished Princess Fiorella would hurry up and get home and take her insane brother away.

'Because I'm not there, I'm here and you're not getting rid of me...' He suddenly frowned. 'Forgive me, I've forgotten your name.'

Seriously? He'd just suggested they get married and he didn't even know her name?

'I don't think you ever knew it,' she said wryly. 'Hester Moss.'

'Hester.' He repeated her name a couple more times softly, turning it over in his mouth as if taking the time to decide on the flavour and then savouring it. 'That's very good.' Another smile curved his mouth. 'I'm Alek.'

'I'm aware of who you are, Your Highness.' And she was not going to let him try to seduce her into complying with his crazy scheme.

Except deep inside her something flipped. A miniscule seed long crushed by the weight of loss and bullying now sparked into a tiny wistful ache for adventure.

Prince Alek was studying her as if he were assessing a new filly for his famous stables. That damned smile flickered around his mouth again and the dimples danced—all teasing temptation. 'I think this could work very well, *Hester.*'

His soft emphasis of her name whispered over her skin. He was so used to getting his way—so handsome, so charming, he was utterly spoilt. Had he not actually heard her say the word no or did he just not believe it was possible that she meant it?

'I think you like a joke,' she said almost hoarsely. 'But I don't want to be a joke.'

His expression tightened. 'You wouldn't be. But this could be fun.'

'I don't need fun.'

'Don't you? Then what do you need?' He glanced back into her bedroom. 'You need money.'

'Do I?' she asked idly.

'Everyone normal needs money.'

Everyone normal? Did he mean not royal? 'I don't, I have sufficient,' she lied.

He watched her unwaveringly and she saw the scepticism clearly in his eyes.

'Besides,' she added shakily, 'I have a job.'

'Working for my sister.'

'Yes.' She cocked her head, perceiving danger in his silken tones. 'Or are you going to have me fired if I keep saying no to you?'

His smile vanished. 'First thing to learn—and there will be a lot to learn—I'm not a total jerk. Why not listen to my proposition in full before jumping to conclusions?'

'It didn't cross my mind you were really serious about this.'

'I really am,' he said slowly, as if he didn't quite believe it of himself either. 'I want you to marry me. I'll be crowned King. You'll live a life of luxury in the palace.' He glanced toward her room before turning back to her. 'You'll want for nothing.'

Did he think her sparse little bedroom was miserable? How dared he assume what she might *want*? She wanted for nothing now—not people or things. Not for herself. Except that wasn't *quite* true—and that little seed stirred again, growing bigger already.

'You don't want to stop and think things through?' she asked.

'I've already thought all the things. This is a good plan.'

'For you, perhaps. But *I* don't like being told what to do,' she said calmly. And she didn't like vapid promises of luxury, or the prospect of being part of something that would involve being around so many *people*.

But the Prince just laughed. 'My sister tells you what to do all the time.'

'That's different. She pays me.'

'And I will pay you more. I will pay you very, *very* well.'

Somehow that just made this 'proposal' so much worse. But, of course, it was the only way this proposal would have ever happened. As a repellent job offer.

He looked amused as he studied her. 'I am talking about a marriage *in name only*, Hester. We don't need to have sex. I'm not asking you to prostitute yourself.'

His brutal honesty shocked her. So did the flood of heat that suddenly stormed along her veins—a torrent of confusion and…other things she didn't wish to examine. She braced, struggling to stay her customary calm self. 'An heir isn't part of the expectation?'

He stiffened. 'Thankfully that is not another onerous legal requirement. We can divorce after a period. I'll then change the stupid law and marry again if I'm ever actually willing. I've years to figure that one out once I'm crowned.'

Hester swallowed. He was clearly not interested in having kids. Nor ever marrying anyone for real. He didn't even try to hide the distaste in his eyes. Too bad for him because providing an heir was going to be part of his job at some point. But not hers.

'We'll marry for no more than a year,' he said decisively. 'Think of it as a secondment. Just a year and then back to normal.'

Back to normal? As the ex-wife of a king? There'd be nothing normal after that. Or of spending a year in his presence as his pretend wife. She was hardly coping with these last ten minutes.

He hadn't even thought to ask if she was single. He'd taken one look at her and assumed everything. And he was right. Which made it worse. Another wave of bitterness swept over her even though she knew it was pathetic. Hester Moss, inconsequential nobody.

'Can you use your country's money to buy yourself a bride?' she blurted bitterly.

'This will be from my personal purse,' he answered crisply. 'Perhaps you aren't aware I'm a successful man in my own right?'

She didn't want to consider all that she knew about him. But it was there, in a blinding neon lights, the harsh reality of Prince Alek's *reputa-*

tion. She couldn't think past it—couldn't believe he could either.

'There's a bigger problem,' she said baldly.

'And that is?'

'You've a very active social life.' She glanced down, unable to hold his gaze as she raised this. 'Am I supposed to have just accepted that?'

'I didn't realise you've been reading my personal diary.'

'I didn't need to,' she said acidly. 'It's all over the newspapers.'

'And you believe everything you read?'

'Are you saying it's not true?'

There was a moment and she knew. It was all *so* true.

'I've not been a monk,' he admitted through gritted teeth. 'But I didn't take advantage of any woman any more than she took advantage of me.' He gazed at her for a long moment and drew in an audible breath. 'Perhaps you've held me at bay. Perhaps I've been hiding my broken heart.'

'By sleeping with anyone willing?' she asked softly, that anger burgeoning again.

'Not *all* of them.' He actually had the audacity to laugh. 'Not even my stamina is that strong.'

Just most of them, then? 'And can you go without that…intimacy for a whole year?'

He stilled completely and stared fixedly at her.

'Plenty of people can and do,' he said eventually. 'Why assume I'm unable to control myself?'

That heat burned her cheeks even hotter. 'It's not the lifestyle you're accustomed to.'

'You'd be amazed what hardships I can handle,' he retorted. 'Will *you* be able to handle it?'

He was well within his rights to question her when she'd done the same to him. But she didn't have to speak the truth. Provoked, she brazenly flung up her chin and snapped, 'Never.'

But he suddenly laughed. 'You're so serene even when you lie.' He laughed again. 'Marry me. Make me the happiest man on earth.'

'If I said yes, it would serve you right,' she muttered.

'Go on, then, Ms Moss,' he dared her softly. 'Put me in my place.'

A truly terrible temptation swirled within her and with it came a terribly seductive image. She shook her head to clear it. She couldn't get mesmerised into madness just because he was unbearably handsome and had humour to boot. 'It's impossible.'

'I think you could do it.' His eyes gleamed and she grew wary of what he was plotting. 'If you don't need money…' he trailed off, his voice lifting with imperceptible disbelief '…then give it to someone who does.'

Hester froze.

His gaze narrowed instantly. 'What's your favourite charity?' He sounded smoothly practical, but she sensed he was circling like a shark, in ever-decreasing circles, having sensed weakness he was about to make his killer move.

'I'll make a massive donation,' he offered. 'Millions. Think of all those worthy causes you could help. All those people. Or is it animals—cats, of course. Perhaps the planet? Your pick. Divide it amongst them all, I don't care.'

'Because you're cynical.' But her heart thudded. Because she'd give the money to people who she knew desperately needed help.

'Actually, I'm not at all,' he denied with quiet conviction. 'If we find ourselves in the position to be able to help others in any way, or to leave the place in a better condition than which we found it, then we should, shouldn't we? It's called being decent.'

He pinned her with that intense gaze of his. Soulful or soul*less*? Her heart beat with painfully strong thuds.

'You can't say no to that, can you?' he challenged her.

He was questioning her humanity? Her compassion? She stared back at him—he had no idea of her history, and yet he'd struck her with this.

'If you don't need it,' he pressed her, 'isn't there someone in your life who does?'

There were very, very few people in her life. But he'd seen. He knew this was the chink in her armour. And while she really wanted to say no again, just to have it enforced for once in his precious life, how could she not say yes?

At the drop-in centre she'd been trying to help a teen mother and her toddler for the past three weeks. Lucia and her daughter, Zoe, were alone and unsupported having been rejected by family and on the move ever since. If someone didn't step in and help them, Lucia was at risk of having Zoe taken and put into care. Hester had given Lucia what spare cash she could and tried to arrange emergency accommodation. She knew too well what it was to be scared and without security or safety or a loving home.

'You're emotionally blackmailing me,' she said lowly, struggling to stop those thoughts from overwhelming her.

'Am I?' He barely breathed. 'Is it working?'

He watched her for another long moment as she inwardly wrestled with the possibilities. She knew how much it mattered for Lucia and Zoe to stay together. Her parents had fought to stay together and to keep her with them and when they'd died she'd discovered how horrible it was to be foisted upon unwilling family. With money came resources and power and freedom.

Prince Alek sent her a surprisingly tentative

smile. 'Come on, Hester.' He paused. 'Wouldn't it be a little bit fun?'

Did she look as if she needed 'fun'? Of course she did. She knew what she looked like. Most of the time she didn't care about it, but right now?

'You like to do the unpredictable.' She twisted her hands together and gripped hard, trying to hold onto reality. 'You delight in doing that.'

'Doesn't everyone like to buck convention sometimes? Not conform to the stereotype others have put them in?'

He was too astute because now she thought of those bullies—her cousins and those girls at school—who'd attacked her looks, her lack of sporting prowess, her lack of *parents*...the ones who'd been horrifically mean.

'I *really* don't want to be used as a joke.' She'd been that before and was sure the world would see their marriage that way—it was how he was seeing it, right? Nothing to be taken seriously. And she was too far from being like any woman he'd make his bride.

'Again, I'm not a jerk. I'll take you seriously and I'll ensure everyone around us does too. I'll make a complete commitment to you for the full year. I promise you my loyalty, honesty, integrity and *fidelity*. I only ask for the same in return. We could be a good team, Hester.' He glanced again at her desk. 'I know you do a good job. Fi raves about you.'

Hester's pride flickered. She did do a good job. And she knew she was too easily flattered. But this was different, this was putting herself in a vulnerable position. This was letting all those people from her past *see* her again. She'd be more visible than ever before—more vulnerable.

But hadn't she vowed not to let anyone hurt her again?

'Working for Princess Fiorella is a good job for me,' she reminded herself as much as informed him. 'I won't be able to come back to it.'

'You won't need to,' he reasoned. 'You'll be in a position to do anything you want. You'll have complete independence. You'll be able to buy your own place, fill it with cats and books about serial killers. All I'm asking for is one year.'

One year was a long time. But what she could do for Lucia and Zoe? She could change their lives *for ever*. If someone had done that for her parents? Or for her? But no one had and she'd spent years struggling. While she was in a better place now, Zoe wasn't.

Hester squared her shoulders. If she could survive what she already had, then she could survive this too. And maybe, with a little change in 'packaging', she could subvert that stereotype those others had placed on her—and yes, wouldn't that be a little 'fun'?

That long-buried seed unfurled, forming the smallest irrepressible bud. An irresistible desire for adventure, a chance impossible to refuse. She couldn't say no when he was offering her the power to change everything for someone so vulnerable. And for herself.

'I think you'll like Triscari,' he murmured easily. 'The weather is beautiful. We have many animals. We're most famous for our horses, but we have cats too...'

She gazed at him, knowing he was wheedling because he sensed success.

'All right,' she said calmly, even as she was inwardly panicking already. 'One year's employment.'

Predatory satisfaction flared in his eyes. Yes. This was a man who liked to get his way. But he was wise enough not to punch the air with an aggressive fist. He merely nodded. Because he'd expected her acquiescence all along, hadn't he?

'It'll cost you,' she added quickly, feeling the sharp edge of danger press.

'All the money?' His smile quirked.

'Yes,' she answered boldly, despite her thundering heart. 'So much money.'

'You have plans.' He sounded dispassionately curious. 'What are you going to do with it?'

'You want your privacy, I want mine,' she snapped. 'If I want to bathe in a tub full of crisp, new dollar bills, that's my prerogative.' She wasn't telling him or anyone. Not even Lucia and Zoe, because she didn't want any of this to blow back on them. This would be a secret gift.

'Wonderful. Let me know when you want them delivered.' He looked amused. 'Shall we shake on it?'

Gravely she placed her hand in his, quelling the shiver inside as he grasped her firmly. He didn't let her go, not until she looked up. The second she did, she was captured by that contrary mix of caution and curiosity and concern in his beautiful eyes. She had the horrible fear they were *full* of soul.

It didn't seem right for him to bow before her and, worse, she couldn't make herself respond in kind, not even to incline her head. She couldn't seem to move—her lungs had constricted. And her heart? That had simply stopped.

'Let's go get married, Hester,' he suggested, his lightness at odds with that ever-deepening intensity of his gaze. 'The sooner the better.'

CHAPTER TWO

ALEK COULDN'T QUITE believe what he'd just established. But that reckless part of him—that sliver of devilishness—felt nothing but euphoria. Here she was. The method by which he'd finally please the courtiers and parliamentarians who'd been pestering him for months. The means by which he'd find his freedom and fulfil his destiny at the same time.

Ms Hester Moss.

Personal assistant. Calm automaton. Perfect wife. Yes, he was going to give his country their most inoffensive, bland Queen. In her navy utility trousers, her crisp white tee shirt, her large-rimmed glasses and her hair in that long, purely functional ponytail at the nape of her neck, she looked least like any royal bride ever. Not tall, not especially slender, not styled and definitely not coated in that sophisticated confidence he was used to. In that sense she was right, she was nothing like the women he usually dated. And that was perfect. Because he didn't want to date her. And she definitely didn't want to date him. This would be a purely functional arrangement. No sex. No complications.

She had something better to offer him. She was self-contained, precise, earnest, and—he'd bet—*dutiful*. She'd be efficient, discreet, courteous and they'd co-exist for this limited time in complete harmony And she wasn't a dragon or a bitch; she seemed too bloodless to be either. Actually, now he thought about it, she struck him as *too* controlled, too careful altogether. Irritation rippled beneath his skin. He knew she judged him—hell, who didn't? But he wanted to scratch the surface and find *her* faults. After all, everyone had flaws and weaknesses. Everyone had something that made their blood boil. He'd seen it briefly when she'd referenced his 'lifestyle', when she'd called him out for being 'spoiled', when she'd felt the need to snap *no* at him.

But he'd just got her to say yes to him and damn if it didn't feel good. Only now he was wondering *why* she wanted the pots of gold.

He could pull her file from security but immediately rejected the idea. His father would never have allowed Fiorella near someone unsuitable, so there could be nothing in her past to cause concern. He'd satisfy his curiosity the old-fashioned way. Face to face. The prospect of breaking through her opaque, glass façade and making her reveal the snippets of herself that she seemed determined to keep secret was surprisingly appealing. The only question was *how* he'd go about it.

Now he had her hand in his and he was gazing into her eyes—a breath away for the first time. Even behind the large-framed glasses, he could appreciate their colour—pure gold, a warm solid hue—and it seemed she wasn't averse to a little smoke and mirrors because she had to be wearing mascara. Her eyelashes were abnormally thick. Heat burned across the back of his neck and slowly swept down his spine, around his chest, skimming lower and lower still. Startled by the unexpected sensation, he tensed, unable to release her cool hand, unable to cease staring into her amazing, leonine eyes.

'Alek?'

He blinked and turned his head. 'Fi.'

His sister was gaping at their linked hands.

He felt a tug and turned back to see awkwardness swarm over Hester's face. Slowly he obeyed her wordless plea and released her hand.

'What are you doing here?' Fiorella stepped forward, her astonishment obvious. 'What's going on?'

He drew a sharp breath and slammed into a snap decision. He would do this with supreme discretion. No one but he and Hester would know the truth and if they could pass the Fifi test here and now, they'd be fine with the rest of the world. 'We didn't intend to surprise you this way,' he said smoothly. 'But Hester and I are engaged.'

'Engaged? To *Hester*?' Fi's eyes bugged. *'No way.'*

'Fi—'

'You don't even *know* each other.' Fi was clearly stunned.

'That's where you're wrong. Again,' he muttered. 'We know each other far better than you think.'

'But...' Fi looked from him to Hester and that frown deepened on her face. 'No way.'

He glanced at Hester and saw she'd paled. She shoved her hands into the horrendously practical pockets of her cotton drill trousers and stood eerily still, her façade determinedly uncrackable.

'Hester?' Fiorella gazed at her assistant, a small frown formed between her brows. 'I know you've been distracted lately and not as available...'

Alek glanced at Hester and saw she'd gone paler still. His instincts were engaged—what had been distracting her? The whisper of vulnerability prickled his senses.

'She works for *me*.' Fifi pulled his attention back with her quiet possessiveness. 'And I don't want you to...mess her around.'

Hester's eyes widened and colour scurried back into her cheeks. But to his astonishment, a pretty smile broke through her tense, expressionless façade. His jaw dropped and for a moment he had the oddest wish that he'd been the one to make her smile like that. She'd suddenly looked luminous and *soft*. But then the smile faded and her self-contained neutrality was restored.

'I'm a big girl, Princess Fiorella,' Hester said in that careful, contained way she had. 'I can take care of myself.'

Alek realised Hester had feared Fi disapproved of *her*. And she was hugely relieved to discover she didn't.

'I know you had no idea,' Hester added as she gestured towards him. 'But we had our reasons for that.'

Instinctively he reached out and clasped her hand back in his. A stunningly strong ripple of possessiveness shimmered through him. Again acting on instinct, he laced his fingers through hers and locked his grip. For the proof in front of Fifi, right?

His sister now stared again at their interlinked hands, her eyes growing round before she flashed a hurt look up at Alek. 'Is this because of that stupid requirement?'

'This is because it is what both your brother and I *want*.'

Hester's faintly husky emphasis on the 'want' tightened his skin.

'I'm so sorry to have kept this from you, but it's been quite…tough.'

'And I'm sorry for the short notice,' Alek added as Hester faltered. 'But I'm taking Hester back with me immediately.'

'To Triscari? Now?' Fi clasped her hands in front of her chest. 'You're for real? Like really for real?'

That light flush swept more deeply across Hester's face as Alek confirmed it with a twinge of regret. His sister was young and unspoiled but he found himself watching Hester more closely for clues as to what was going on beneath her still exterior.

'It's like a fairy tale,' Fifi breathed. 'Oh, Alek, this is wonderful.'

Hester's hand quivered in his and he tightened his hold.

'You're really leaving right away?' Fi asked.

'It's been difficult,' Alek said honestly. 'It's best we get back to Triscari. There's a lot for Hester to take in.'

Worry dulled the delight in Fi's eyes.

'It's okay. Everything's in your diary and you can always text me with any problems,' Hester said earnestly. 'I can keep answering your correspondence—that's the bulk of what I do for you and there's no reason why I can't continue.'

Alek bit his tongue to stop himself interrupting with all the reasons why she wasn't going to be able to keep working for his sister.

'Are you sure?' Fi's relief was audible.

'Hester can help train someone up to take over from her quite quickly.' He sent Hester a shamelessly wicked smile. 'After all, you'll be busy managing your own mail shortly.'

A mildly alarmed look flickered in her eyes before she smiled politely back.

'Well.' Fi drew breath. 'I have to go, I'm late to meet my friend. I only called in to tell Hester I need her to...never mind. I can do it. I'll leave you to...go.' She glanced again between him and Hester. 'I still can't believe it.'

Fi stepped in and Alek gave her a one-armed hug.

He met Hester's gaze over the top of Fi's head and saw the glint of amusement in her eyes. She was very good at managing her emotions and at managing a volatile Fiorella. A volatility he knew he had in common with his sister on occasion.

When Fi left, he released Hester's hand—with a surprising amount of reluctance.

'Thank you,' he said. He needed to focus on the important things. Like fabricating their story. 'You're good at lying.'

'I'm good at saying what's necessary for self-preservation,' she replied. 'That's a different skill.'

His senses sharpened. Self-preservation? Why was that?

'You really want us to maintain this "relationship" in front of Princess Fiorella?' she asked too calmly.

'For now.' He nodded. 'I don't want to risk any inadvertent revelations and I don't want her to worry.'

'She's your sister, she's going to be concerned about your *happiness*.'

'I thought she seemed more worried about you than me.' He shot her an ironic glance.

'She doesn't need to worry about me.' Hester gazed down at her desk. 'I'm fine. I can handle anything.'

He had the odd feeling she could but that didn't mean that she *should*. 'It seems the pretence is under way, Hester. This is your last chance to back out.'

She was silent for a moment, but then lifted her serene face to his. 'No, let's do this. You should be crowned.'

Really? He didn't think she was in this for *his* benefit. She'd become rich; that was the real reason, wasn't it? Except he didn't think it was. What did she plan to do with the money?

He frowned. It shouldn't matter, it wasn't his business.

But what had she been so 'distracted' with lately? Not a man, or she'd not have said yes to him. He'd bet it was someone else, someone she wanted the money for.

He huffed out a breath and willed his curiosity to ebb. He didn't need to know any more. She was palace employed, therefore palace perfect. Contained, aloof, efficient. She even maintained a polite distance from Fi, who he knew was physically demonstrative. He now realised part of Fi's shock—and reason for her eventual belief—had been because he and Hester were *touching*. Fiorella hadn't hugged Hester when she'd left. He was sure the reserve came from Hester—strictly observing her role as employee, not confidante or friend. Doubtless she was all about 'professional boundaries', or something. It was evident in the way she dressed too. The utilitarian clothes and sensible black canvas shoes were almost a services uniform from the nineteen-forties. But her hourglass figure couldn't quite be hidden even by those ill-tailored trousers. Her narrow waist and curving hips held all the promise of soft, lush pillow for a man...that *stability* she'd made him think of.

But she made him think about other things too—like why did she live in that prison-like cell of a bedroom? Why was it so lacking in anything personal other than a mangy stray cat, a broken wooden box and a pile of second-hand books?

She was like a walled-off puzzle with several

pieces missing. Happily, Alek quite enjoyed puzzles and he had a year to figure her out. Too easy—and there was no reason they couldn't be *friends*. He could ignore the unexpected flares of physical interest. If his desperate speed-dating of the last month had proven anything to him, it was that the last thing he wanted was anything remotely like a real relationship. Definitely not a true marriage. Not for a very long time. As for that vexed issue providing his kingdom with an heir…that he was just going to put off for as long as possible. Somehow he'd find a way to ensure any child of his didn't suffer the same constraints he had.

'We should make plans.' He moved forward to her desk. 'I need to contact the palace. You need to pack.' He glanced over to where she stood worryingly still. 'Or…?'

'How are we going to end this?' she asked pensively. 'In a year. What will we say?'

He was relieved she wasn't pulling out on him already. 'I'll take the blame.'

'No. Let me,' she said quietly. 'You're the King.'

'No.' He refused to compromise on this. 'You'll be vilified.'

Double standards abounded, wrong as it was, and he wasn't having her suffer in any way because of this. He'd do no harm. And she was doing him a huge favour.

'I don't want to be walked over,' she said a little unevenly. '*I'll* do the stomping. Keep your reputation. Mine doesn't matter.'

He stared at her. She stood more still than ever—defensively prim, definitely prickly—and yet she wanted to be reckless in that?

'You'd sacrifice everything,' he tried to inform her gently.

'Actually, I'll sacrifice nothing,' she contradicted. 'I don't care what they say about me.'

No one didn't care. Not anyone human, anyway. And he'd seen her expression change drastically when Fi had returned, so Hester was definitely human. She'd been terrified of his sister's reaction—of her disapproval. Which meant she liked and cared about Fi. And she cared about doing the stomping.

Now he studied her with interest, opting not to argue. He'd had all the wins so far, so he could let this slide until later because he was totally unhappy with the idea of her taking the responsibility for their marriage 'breakdown'.

'We'll finalise it nearer the time.'

She softened fractionally.

'You know they'll want all the pomp and ceremony for this wedding.' He rolled his eyes irreverently, wanting to make her smile again. 'All the full regalia.'

'You really don't think much of your own traditions, do you?'

'Actually, I care greatly about my country and my people and *most* of our customs. But I do find the feathers on the uniform impede my style a little.'

'Feathers?' She looked diverted and suddenly, as he'd hoped, her soft smile peeked out. Followed by a too-brief giggle. 'So, you really mean smoke and mirrors?'

'It's a little ridiculous, I'm afraid.' He nodded with a grin. 'But not necessarily wrong.'

'Okay. Smoke. Mirrors. Feathers.' But she seemed to steel herself and shot him a searching look. 'You don't think everyone will know the wedding is only for the coronation?'

'Not if we convince them otherwise.'

'And how do we do that?'

'We just convinced Fi, didn't we?'

'She's a romantic.'

'So we give them romance.' Fire flickered along his limbs and he tensed to stop himself stepping closer and seeing what kind of 'romance' he could spontaneously conjure with her. What he might discover beneath her serene but strong veneer. 'Trust me, Hester. We'll make this believable. We'll make it brilliant.' He cocked his head. 'I think with some work we can look like a couple in love.'

Her eyes widened. 'But there's no need for us to *touch*.' She sounded almost breathless with horror. 'Nothing like that. We'll be very circumspect, won't we?'

Alek suppressed his laugh. His officials were going to love her, given how much they loathed his usual less than circumspect affairs. And if she presented this shy, blushing bride act to the public, she'd melt all hearts.

'You mean no public displays of affection?' he queried more calmly than he felt.

'That's right.'

Was she serious? 'None at *all*?'

He keenly watched her attempt to maintain her unruffled expression, but tell-tale colour surged over her skin and ruined her proud attempt. But she didn't reply and he realised she was utterly serious. So what about *private* displays of affection?

The fierce desire to provoke her came from nowhere and astounded him. The ways he'd make her blush all over? To make her smile and sigh and *scream*?

The immediate cascade of thoughts was so hot and heady, he tensed all over again. It was just the challenge, right? She'd initially told him no with unapologetic bluntness, while excoriating his social life. Now she reckoned she didn't want him to touch her?

Okay, no problem.

Yet surely he wasn't the only one feeling this shocking chemistry? The magnetic pull was too strong to be one-sided. Her colour deepened as the silence stretched and thickened. Of course she felt it, he realised, feeling a gauche fool. It was the whole reason for her complete blushathon.

Hester stared as he hesitated for what felt like for ever. Her whole body felt on fire—with utter and absolute mortification—but this was something she needed not just to clarify, but to make certain—iron-clad in their agreement. It suddenly seemed *essential*.

'Okay,' he agreed, but amusement flitted around his mouth. 'I wasn't about to suggest we practise or anything.'

'Good.' She finally breathed out. 'That would just be stupid.'

'Indeed. I don't need to practise. I know how to kiss.'

Hester didn't quite know how to respond. She wasn't about to admit how totally lacking in kissing experience she was. That heat beat all over her body, but she counted breaths in and out, to restore outward calm at least. Inside she was still frying.

'Because, just so you know, we will have to kiss. Twice, if you can bring yourself to agree.' He gazed at her steadily. 'During the wedding service, which will, of course, be live-streamed.

We'll need to kiss after the commitment during the ceremony and once again on the steps outside the church afterwards.'

'Live-streamed?' Her lungs constricted. 'From a church?'

'In the palace chapel, yes. It's just the part we're both playing, Hester.'

The palace chapel? It really was the stuff of fairy-tale fiction. As long as she remembered that was all it was, then she could go through with it, right? As long as she remembered what she could do for Lucia and Zoe.

'Two kisses,' she conceded briefly.

She was sure they'd be chaste pecks, given they were going to be live-streamed and all. Not even the outrageous Prince Alek would put on a raunchy show for the world with his convenient bride. There was no need for him to ever know she'd never been kissed before.

'Do you think I can hold your hand at the banquet afterwards? Look at you? Smile?'

He was teasing her so she answered with even more determined seriousness. 'Depending on the circumstances, I might even smile back.'

'Depending on the circumstances?' he echoed idly. 'There's a challenge.'

But he sat down at her desk, grabbed a blank piece of paper, borrowed one of her favourite pens and began writing. She watched, fascinated as the paper filled with small squares and a task or reminder beside each. Efficiency, list-making and prioritising? Who'd have thought? After a few moments he studied the list and nodded to himself before pulling out his phone and tapping the screen.

'Good news, Marc. I'm to be married after all. I know you've had the wedding plans in place for months so now you can press "go",' he said with a bitter-edged smile. 'We'll journey home this afternoon.' He paused for a long moment. 'You think that's achievable? Is that long enough for—?' He paused again. 'You flatter me, Marc, but if you're sure.' A few moments later he rang off. 'We're getting married in ten days and the coronation will take place in the week after.'

'Ten days?' Hester echoed.

'I know, sooner than I'd have thought too. But it seems to have been planned since before I was born. It's going to be a state holiday apparently.' He scribbled more items on his ever-increasing list. 'They've got plans for everything—processions, funerals, baptisms.' He glanced across at her with a laughing grin. 'My obituary is already written. They just update it every so often.'

'You're kidding.'

'No. They're prepared for everything. I think they thought I'd get killed in a plane crash or something a few years ago.' He suddenly chuckled. 'Don't look so shocked.'

'It just seems...' She trailed off, wary of expressing her thoughts. But it seemed sad somehow, to have your life so meticulously planned, documented, constrained. Was it so surprising he'd rebelled against it?

'Don't you have every eventuality covered in your management of Fi's correspondence?' He gestured at her immaculate desk. 'I'm assuming you're a lists and contingencies person.'

'Well, yes, but—'

'They just have more lists than you.' He gazed down at his list. 'You'll need a wedding dress. It would be diplomatic if you choose a Triscarian designer. Would that be tolerable?'

'Of course,' she mumbled, but a qualm of panic struck. What had she been thinking? How could she pull off a live-streamed wedding with millions of people watching? Every last one would pick apart, not just her outfit, but every aspect of her appearance. She wasn't a leggy beautiful brunette like Princess Fiorella. She was on the shorter, wider sides of average—as her aunt had so often commented when comparing her to her gazelle-like, mean cousins.

She took a breath and squared her shoulders. She *didn't* care. She'd resolved long ago never to care again. Because the simple fact was she could never live up to the expectation or never please all of them, so why worry about *any*?

'My assistant will arrange for some samples to be brought to the palace.' He wrote yet another item in his harsh scrawl.

'There's not much time to make a dress or adjustments in ten days.' There wasn't much time to get her head around anything, let alone everything.

'They'll have a team. We'll do some preparation as well, how to pose for photos and the like.'

How to *what*? 'You mean you're going to put me through some kind of princess school?'

'Yes.' He met her appalled gaze with laughter. 'There'll be lots of cameras. It can be blinding at first.'

'Perhaps Princess Fiorella can guide me,' she suggested hopefully.

'*I* will,' he replied firmly. 'Fi needs to meet her obligations here. She'll join us only for the ceremony.'

'But it's okay for me to walk out on her right away?'

'Your obligations to me and to Triscari now take precedence.' He added something else to his endless list.

Hester glanced about the room, suddenly thinking about all the things *she* was going to need to achieve. 'I'll have to—'

'Find someone to feed the cat.' He nodded and wrote that down too.

'Yes,' she muttered, internally touched that he'd remembered.

'At my expense, of course,' he added. 'Do you have other work obligations we need to address?'

'I can sort it.' She didn't flatter herself that she was indispensable. No one was. She could disappear from the college and very few people would notice. She'd disappeared before no trouble at all. But she was going to need to sort out Lucia. 'Um…' She cleared her throat. 'I'm going to need…'

'The money?' He lifted his head to scrutinise her and waggled his pen between forefinger and thumb. 'You want your first bathtub full of dollar bills?'

The intensity in his eyes made it hard to keep her equilibrium.

'A few bundles would be good,' she mumbled.

He tore another piece of paper from the pad and put it on the opposite side of the desk in front of her. 'Write down the details and I'll have it done.'

He didn't ask more about why she wanted it. She half hoped he understood it wasn't for her.

'What family would you like to invite?' he asked. 'You can have as many as you like. Write the list and I'll have them arrange invitations, transport and accommodation.'

She froze, her pen hovering just above the paper. Family?

She eventually glanced at him. He'd stopped writing and was watching her as he waited for her reply with apparently infinite patience. She wanted to look away from his eyes, but couldn't. And she'd said this so many times before, this shouldn't be different. But it was. Her breathing quickened. She just needed to say it. Rip the plaster off. That way was best. 'My parents died when I was a child.'

He didn't bat an eyelid. 'Foster parents, then? Adoptive? Extended family?'

She swallowed to push back the rising anxiety. 'Do I have to invite them?'

His gaze remained direct and calm. 'If you don't invite anyone, there will be comment. I'm used to comment, so that doesn't bother me. But if it will bother you, then I'd suggest inviting but then keeping them at a distance. That would be the diplomatic route that the courtiers will prefer.'

'What would you prefer?' Her heart banged against her ribcage.

'I want you to do whatever will help you get through the day.'

That understated compassion shook her serenity and almost tempted her to confide in him.

But she barely thought about her 'family'. She couldn't bear to. And she hadn't seen them in years. 'If they do come, will I have to spend time much with them...?'

He looked thoughtful and then the corners of his eyes crinkled. 'I can be very possessive and dictatorial.'

'You mean you'll abuse your power?' She couldn't supress another giggle.

'Absolutely.' His answering grin was shameless and charming and pleased. 'That's what you'd expect from me, right?'

Her heart skipped. 'The perks of being a prince...'

But her own smile faded as she considered the ramifications. She'd never wanted to see those people again, but this was an extremely public wedding. If she didn't invite them there'd be more than mere speculation: journalists would sniff about for stories. If they dug deep old wounds might be opened, causing more drama. Anyway, her extended family liked nothing more than status, so if she invited them to the royal wedding of the decade, they'd be less likely to say anything. They'd never admit they'd disowned her father, spurned her pregnant mother, and caused her teenage parents to run away like some modern-day Romeo and Juliet. They'd never admit that they'd only taken her in after the accident for 'the look of it'. Or that they'd never let her forget how she was the unplanned and unwanted 'trash' who'd ruined the perfect plan they'd had for her father's life.

'Do you have someone you'd like to escort you down the aisle?' he asked.

She noted with a wry smile that he didn't suggest she be given away. 'It's fine, I'll do that alone.' She looked at the paper in front of her. 'But perhaps Princess Fiorella might act as bridesmaid?' She wasn't sure if it was appropriate, but there really wasn't anyone else she could think of.

'That would work very well.'

'Perfect for your pining heart narrative,' she joked to cover the intensity of the discussion.

'The media will seize on this as soon as they hear anything,' Alek said solemnly. 'They will pry into your private life, Hester. Are you prepared for that?'

'It's fine.' She went back to writing her own list to avoid looking at him. 'They can say what they like, print what they like.'

'No skeletons in the closet?' he queried gently. 'It wouldn't bother me if there were. Heaven knows I have them.' She heard his smile in his voice before it dropped lower. 'But I wouldn't want you to suffer.'

She shook her head and refused to look up at him again. 'It's fine.'

'There are no ex-boyfriends who are going to sell their stories about you to the press?'

Her blush built but she doggedly kept looking down. Why did he have to press this? He didn't need to know.

'They're harder on women,' he said huskily. 'Wrong as that is.'

'There are no skeletons. I was lonely as a teenager. I wasn't really close to anyone.' Uncomfortable, she glanced up to assure him and instantly regretted it because she was caught in the coal-black depths of his eyes. 'My life to date has been very boring,' she said flatly. 'There's literally nothing to write about.'

Nothing in her love life anyway. She couldn't break free of his unwavering gaze and slowly that heat curled within her—embarrassment, right? But she also felt an alarming temptation to lean closer to him. Instead she froze. 'Is it a problem?'

'Not at all.'

She forced herself to focus on listing the details he'd asked for, rather than the strange sensations burgeoning within her.

This marriage was a few months of adventure. She had to treat it like that. If she'd been crazy enough to say yes to such an outlandish, impulsive proposal, she might as well go all the way with it. 'Will your assistant be able to find me a hairdresser?' She pushed past her customary independence and made herself ask for the help she needed. 'And maybe some other clothes...'

'You'd like that?'

She glanced up again and saw he was still studying her intently.

'All the smoke and mirrors?' she joked lamely again. 'I'd like all the help I can get to pull this off.'

'Then I'll have it arranged. Write down your size and I'll have some things brought to the plane.'

Heat suffused her skin again but she added it to her list before pushing the paper towards him. 'I think that's everything.'

'Good,' he said briskly. 'Start packing. I have several calls to make.'

Relieved, she escaped into her small bedroom. With an oblique reference to 'a family matter', her volunteer co-ordinator at the drop-in centre expressed regret but understanding. It took only a moment to open an anonymous email account from which she could make the arrangements for her support for Lucia. Packing her belongings took only a moment too. She picked up the antique wooden box Alek had touched and carefully put it into the small backpack she'd used when she'd run away all those years ago. Her clothes fitted easily into the one small suitcase she'd acquired since.

'That's everything?' He stared in frank amazement at her suitcase when she returned to the lounge.

'I don't need much.'

'You're going to need a little more than that.' He reached out to take the case from her. 'It's probably good that we leave before Fi gets back. Saves on all the questions she'll have been stockpiling over the last hour.'

But Hester didn't follow him as he headed towards the door. 'Are you absolutely certain about this, Your Highness?'

He turned back to face her. 'Of course I'm certain,' he said with absolute princely arrogance. 'And you need to call me Alek.'

'Okay.' She hoisted her backpack and walked towards the door.

But he blocked her path. 'Do it now. Practise so it slips off your tongue naturally. Call me Alek.'

'I will.'

He still didn't move to let her past. A frisson of awareness, danger, defiance, shivered within her as she defiantly met his gaze.

'Say, *Alek is wonderful*. Now,' he commanded.

She glared harder at him. 'Alek is bossy.'

'Good enough.' He stepped back, the distance between them enabling her to breathe again. But his slow smile glinted with full wickedness. 'For now.'

CHAPTER THREE

SWIFT WASN'T THE word for Alek's modus operandi. When he'd decided something, he moved. Fast.

'You're very used to getting your own way,' Hester said as she followed him downstairs out of the campus residence she'd called home for the last three years.

'You think?' He shot her a look. 'I have the feeling I might not get everything quite on my terms for a while.'

'Is that such a threat?' Without thinking, another small smile sparkled free.

'Not at all,' he denied with relish. 'I enjoy a challenge.'

Oh, she wasn't a *challenge*. She was never going to be some kind of toy for this notorious playboy. But she forgot any flattening reply she was mulling when she saw the entourage waiting outside. Large, almost armoured vehicles were staffed by a phalanx of ferociously physical suited and booted men armed with earpieces and dark eyewear and who knew what else beneath the black fabric of their jackets. Alek guided her directly to the middle car. She was absurdly glad of its size and comfort, air conditioning and sleek silence. Her pulse hammered as they drove through the streets and she tried to stop herself snatching looks at him.

Lucia and Zoe will be secure and together.

That was what she needed to focus on. *Not his dimples.*

But her nerves mounted. The fluttering in her tummy was because she'd never flown in a plane before, that was all.

That's not all.

This whole thing was insane. She needed to tell him she'd made a mistake. Back out and beg him to help that family—surely he would once he heard about Lucia's struggle?

'Okay?' Alek was watching her with astute amusement.

She thought about Lucia and Zoe again. She thought about living on a warm island for a while. She thought about full financial freedom and independence for the rest of her life.

'Okay.' She nodded.

They went through a side door of the airport terminal. A uniformed woman escorted them directly to the plane.

'Everyone is aboard?' Alek asked.

'Yes, sir. We're cleared for departure as soon as you're seated.'

Hester paused in the doorway and frowned. This wasn't a small private jet like ones she'd seen in the movies. This was a commercial airliner. Except it wasn't. There weren't rows of cramped seats and masses of people. This was a lounge with sofas and small armchairs around wooden tables. Accented with back-lit marble and mirrors, it was so beautiful, it was like a *hotel*.

She gaped. 'Is this really a plane?'

He smiled as he gestured for her to sit in one of the wide white leather armchairs and showed her where the seat belt hid. 'I'll give you the tour once we're in the air. Can I take your bag?'

'Can I keep it with me?' Her box was in there and it contained her most precious things.

'In this compartment, here.' He stowed it and took the seat opposite hers. 'I've arranged for a stylist to fly with us, so you can make a start, and I've had an assistant pull together a report on some key staffers so you can get ahead of the game on who's who at the palace.' He pulled a tablet from another hidden compartment. 'I don't find the palace intimidating, but I was born there so it's normal for me.' He shrugged his shoulders.

She nodded, unable to speak or smile. It was enough effort to stay calm. Was she really about to leave the country? About to marry a man who was destined to become a king? About to launch into the air in a giant tin can?

'Nervous?'

'Of course,' she muttered honestly. 'But once I've done some preparation I'll feel better.'

His pilots would have years of expertise behind them. She breathed carefully, managing her emotions. After a while she could glance out of the window. They'd climbed steeply and now the plane levelled out.

'Follow me,' Alek said, unfastening his seat belt.

She fumbled and he reached across and undid her belt for her.

'Are you—?'

'I'm fine,' she interrupted and quickly stood, taking a pace away from him. He was too close and she was unable to process the spaciousness. 'Are all private planes this big?'

'No,' he smirked. 'Mine's the biggest.'

'Of course it is,' she muttered. 'Your ego could handle nothing less.'

'Miaow.' He laughed. 'I see why you're friends with that grumpy cat.'

Beyond the private lounge he pointed out a bedroom suite—with more marble and mirrors—then led her through another lounge to another cabin that was more like the business-class seating she'd seen in the movies. Half the seats were full—several of those suited bodyguard types, then others who looked like assistants. As she and Alek neared, they all scrambled to stand.

'Please.' Alek smiled and gestured for them to remain seated. 'Is your team ready, Billie?'

'Of course, Your Highness.' A slim jeans-clad woman stood, as did another couple of people.

'This is Hester,' Alek said briefly when they were back in the second lounge. 'I'll leave you to introduce your team. Please take good care of her.' He sent her a small mocking smile and headed back to the front of the plane.

That was it? There were no instructions? She had no idea what she was supposed to do.

'We're here to help you, Ms Moss,' Billie said confidently.

And there was indeed a team. A hairdresser, a make-up artist, a beautician and a tailor. They were doing a wonderful job of hiding their curiosity but it was so strong she could almost taste it.

'Would you mind if we untie your hair?'

Hester paused. She had to trust Alek's choice, and in their professionalism. 'Of course.' She pulled the elastic tie to free her ponytail. 'I just need you to make me presentable as consort to the King.'

All four of them just stared at her, making her feel awkward.

'That's not going to be a problem,' Billie replied after endless seconds. 'Not a problem.'

She didn't pretend she could reach for anything more than presentable. But she'd been around Princess Fiorella long enough to understand a few tricks. Tailored clothing and some polish could make her passable.

'We have some dresses,' Billie said. 'Would you try them on first so I can make alterations while you're with the beautician?'

'Of course, thank you.' Hester watched, stunned, as Billie unzipped several garment bags while Jon the hairdresser began laying out his tools on the table. 'You must have run to get all this together so quickly.'

'An assignment like this?' A huge smile spread across Jon's face. 'Once in a lifetime.'

Once in a lifetime was right. And it was an assignment for her as much as it was for them. She could learn to do what was necessary, she could even excel in some areas. But she definitely needed help with this. She'd never had the desire to look good before; frankly she'd never wanted people to notice her. Blending in was safer. Hiding was safer still.

But now people were going to be looking so she needed armour. That was what clothing and make-up could be, right?

Hester spent the best part of an hour turning

this way and that and holding still while Billie pinned her waist and hem. The fabrics were so soft and sleek, slowly her trepidation ebbed and she actually began to enjoy herself.

'Now I have your measurements, I can get you some more when we land in Triscari,' Billie said.

Hester glanced at the pile of clothes laid out on the table. 'Do I need more?'

'Much more.' Billie swiftly hung the dresses. 'It's not all photo shoots and public engagements. You'll still have day-to-day life at the palace.'

Hester bit back a nervous giggle. It sounded fantastical and her usual navy utility trousers weren't exactly palace proper. 'Okay, some more casual items would be wonderful. And…' she fought back her blush '…perhaps some new underwear.'

'Leave it with me.' Billie smiled.

Hester smiled shyly. As the beautician waxed, plucked, buffed and massaged her, hours of flight time passed by and she was able to avoid conversation by studying the information on the tablet Alek had given her. Wrapped in a white fluffy robe, she sat in one of the chairs in the boardroom while Jon settled a towel around her shoulders.

She'd never coloured her hair or had any sort of stylish cut because she'd never been able to afford it. So now she sat still for hours as Jon and his assistant hovered over her while Billie hand-sewed alterations to the stunning dresses.

'Okay,' Jon said. 'Take as long as you like in the shower and then we'll get to drying it.'

'Shower? Seriously?' On an airplane?

'Apparently so.' Jon grinned. 'I've been in some planes...but this?'

The biggest and the best. She bit back her grimace.

As she dressed, Hester tried not to wonder what Alek would think of her make-over. He didn't need to find her *attractive*. She just needed to pass inspection.

But inside, she felt oddly different. There was something sensual about her smooth skin, rendered silky by the luxuriant lotions the beautician had rubbed in. For the first time in her life she felt pampered—almost precious.

Alek sprawled back in the recliner, absurdly satisfied with the day's events. He'd gone from frustrated and angry to being in complete control of the situation. Flying off last minute to vent to Fi after another monster row with his chief advisor, Marc, had turned out to be the best idea he'd ever had.

He'd forgotten all about his sister's prim secretary but she was perfect for this assignment. It didn't matter if she wasn't the most beautiful bride the world had ever seen because she was, after all, the one student his father had approved of. Back when Alek had been fighting to get his irascible control-freak father to allow Fiorella to study overseas, he'd come up with the idea of having an approved older student act as a mentor. His father had selected Hester from the pile of student records. So what better temporary wife could Alek produce now? The irony of it delighted him. And not having any emotional entanglement would make this 'marriage' wonderfully straightforward.

Though her determined reserve still fuelled his curiosity. He suspected she was more inexperienced than he'd first realised, but she had a smart head on her shoulders and it was insulting of him to think she couldn't handle this. She was a tough, brave little cookie.

His curiosity deepened as he wondered what personal fire she'd been through to make her so. Because there had to have been something. Why else had she been less than enthusiastic to invite what little family she had left?

He thought again about that barren little bedroom. There was minimalist simplicity and there was plain sad. He knew she had no education debt because she'd been on a scholarship and worked her way through her degree. She was clearly frugal and knew how to live on only a little. Yet she'd wanted a bundle of money in a hurry. Maybe one day she'd tell him why. Though he had the extraordinary inclination to make her tell him sooner. How would he get her to do that? She was so reticent he'd have to tease it out of her. He eased further back in the chair, enjoying the possibilities when the door opened. He glanced up as a goddess walked into his lounge.

Hester Moss.

At least he thought it was Hester. His brain had suddenly been starved of oxygen and he had to blink a couple of times and force his slack jaw actually to suck in a hit of air before he could quite believe his eyes.

'Do I pass?' She gestured to her outfit in an offhand way, her gaze not quite meeting his. 'Am I ready for the media onslaught?'

Her glasses were gone. Her hair was loose. Her baggy, boring clothing had hopefully been consigned to an incinerator because he only wanted her to wear items that fitted her as gorgeously as this dress did. He noticed all these things, but somehow he couldn't actually *think*. He could only stare.

Her expression pinched. 'That much of a difference, huh?'

'We're arriving early—they won't get much in the way of pictures,' he muttered almost incoherently before clearing his throat and reaching for his glass of water.

'Are you saying I just sat through an hour-long hair-drying session for nothing?' She finally looked him directly in the eyes.

'Not for nothing.' Oddly breathless, he detangled the tie in his tongue. 'I think it looks lovely.'

'Oh, that makes it so worth it.' She sat down in the recliner next to his. 'Lovely.'

He grinned, appreciating the lick of sarcasm in her tone. He'd deserved it with that inane comment, but he could hardly be honest. He didn't even want to face that raw and uncontrollable response himself.

Her unruffled composure had swiftly returned and he ached to scrape away that thin veneer because the leonine spark in her eyes a second ago had looked—

'Can you see without the glasses?' he muttered.

'Well enough. Just don't ask me to read my own handwriting,' she quipped.

He stared, leaning closer. 'Your eyelashes are—'

'Weird. I know.'

Her increase in visible tension was so small you'd have to be paying close attention to notice. Fortunately, Alek was paying extremely close attention.

'It's a genetic thing,' she said dismissively, but intriguingly her fingers had curled into fists. 'Don't pull an eyelash out to check they're real.'

As if he'd ever think to do that. Whoever would? 'I believe you.' He forced his stiff face into a smile.

Had someone done that to her in the past? He blinked in disbelief. They really were the thickest, most lush lashes he'd ever seen. 'And your transformation hasn't been a waste of time. We need a portrait shot to go with the media release.'

'You want to take that now?' She looked startled. 'You have a professional photographer on board too, don't you?' She nodded to herself. 'Unreal.'

He chuckled, appreciating the light relief. 'You'll get used to it.'

He buzzed for the photographer, who bounded in with more enthusiasm than usual and keenly listened as Alek explained what he wanted.

'Okay, we can use the white background over here,' the photographer said. 'What about the engagement ring?'

'We'll display that later,' Alek answered swiftly. 'Work around it for now.'

'We can do head and shoulders, but then some relaxed shots—more modern, arty, from the side—'

'Whatever you think,' Alek interrupted. 'Just get them as quickly as you can.'

Hester looked so stiff and uncomfortable, Alek had to suppress both his smile and frustration.

He could think of one way of helping her relax but he didn't think she'd appreciate it. Besides, he'd ruled that out, hadn't he? He'd glibly assured her that of course he could be celibate for a year.

A *year*. The term hit him with the force of an asteroid.

'You *will* get used to it, Hester,' he repeated to reassure her.

But he was the one facing the grim reality of his impetuous decision. No sex. No touching. Just a measly two kisses—what did he think he was, twelve? And did he really think he was in 'complete control' of the situation? Because somehow, something had changed. It had only been a few hours and he was already seeing Hester in a new light. Was he so shallow it was all about the make-over? Or, worse, was it a case of wanting what was off limits—as if he were some spoilt child?

But as he stood next to her his temperature rose. He never sweated through photo sessions; he was too used to them. But she was close enough for him to catch her scent and she seemed to be glowing and it wasn't just the make-up. His fingers itched to touch and see if her skin was as silky soft as it looked.

'Can we try it with you looking at each other?' The photographer sounded frazzled. 'Um…yes, like that.'

Alek gazed at her upturned face. He couldn't think for the life of him why he'd thought her anything less than stunning. She wasn't just beautiful, she was striking. Her golden eyes with those incredible lashes? Her lush pouting lips? That infuriating serenity and stillness of her very self? He couldn't resist putting a careful hand on her waist and drawing her a little closer. He heard the slight catch in her breath but she didn't frown.

'Better,' the photographer muttered. 'Do you think you might be able to smile?'

Alek glanced up from his appallingly lustful stare at her lips to her eyes and amusement flashed between them. He chuckled the same split second she did. And there it was—that soft, enchanting smile he'd not seen enough of. A hot, raw tsunami swept through him at the sight. He wanted more of it.

'Yes!'

Now the photographer sounded far too ecstatic for Alek's liking.

'We'll get changed for the next few shots.' He wanted to be alone with her. He wanted to make her smile again and he didn't want witnesses.

'Good idea.' Hester bit her lip and walked from the room.

Alek automatically followed her into the bedroom, unbuttoning his shirt as he went. 'What colour are—?'

'Oh!' She started and then stared bug-eyed at his chest.

Her eyes grew so round he almost preened as he shrugged his shirt all the way off.

'Is there a problem?' He couldn't help teasing her. But he was beginning to realise the real problem was all his.

No sex for a year?

'I n-need to get changed,' she stammered.

'So get changed.' With exaggerated civility he bowed and then turned his back to her and unlocked the wardrobe for a fresh shirt.

'This is your bedroom?' she choked. 'I'm so sorry, I didn't realise when we put all the clothes...'

'I don't mind, Hester.'

But it was obvious *she* minded very much. All that efficient poise of hers had vanished and he couldn't help enjoying the moment. It was because of *him*.

'Let me know when it's safe to turn around again,' he offered with a self-mocking smile. He'd prove his 'gentleman' credentials—to *himself* as much as to her.

The following silence was appallingly long. He waited, his new shirt buttoned up all the damn way, for what felt like decades for her to give him the all-clear.

'Um…' She finally coughed. 'Would you mind helping me with the zip?'

Oh, was that the problem? 'Sure.' Smothering a laugh, he turned, only to freeze at the sight of her smooth bare back. A gorgeous expanse of creamy skin was edged by the curling sweep of her voluminous golden brown hair—inviting him closer, to touch. Instead he carefully took the dress in the tips of his fingers so as not to inadvertently touch her skin. To prove his restraint to himself. Slowly he pulled the zip up, hiding her from his hungry eyes again. The desire to lean closer, to touch where he had no permission, almost overwhelmed him. By the time he finished the simple task he could barely breathe. He stepped back, coldly furious with himself. Damn if he didn't need to clear his head.

At that moment she turned and he glimpsed fire gleaming in her eyes. That barely hidden blaze of desire slammed the brakes on his breathing all over again.

'You look…' He couldn't think of an adjective—he could only think of action. Impossible action.

'Let's finish this,' she muttered, quickly turning to leave the room.

'Right.' He'd never been rendered speechless before and it took him several minutes to catch his breath. Several minutes in which he had to look into a camera and smile as if this were the happiest day of his life. And then he just gave up. 'Give us a second.'

He took Hester by the hand and walked her down to the other end of the lounge.

'You get sick of it,' she said.

'Utterly,' he admitted, so happy to see her sweet smile flash instantly.

'It must be intense, knowing absolutely everyone around is watching you all the time.'

'You learn to tune it out.'

'And pretend it's normal?' She glanced away, her smile impish as she took in the artwork adorning the plane's interior. 'As if any of this is normal?'

'Well…' he shrugged '…it is normal for me.' He nudged her chin so she looked back at him. 'It bothers you?'

To his gratification, she leaned a little closer as she shook her head, her gaze locked on his.

'That looks amazing.' A masculine voice interrupted from a distance.

Alek froze. He'd completely forgotten the photographer was still down the other end of the lounge. The startled look in Hester's face revealed she'd forgotten too and the half-laugh that escaped from her glossy pout was the sexiest thing he'd ever heard. Smiling back, he pulled her close on pure instinct. The temptation to test the softness of her lips stormed through his reason. Time stopped as he stared into her eyes, trying to read her soft heat and stillness. Could he coax her into—?

'So perfect,' the photographer muttered.

'Enough,' Alek snapped, enraged by the second intrusion. 'We'll be landing soon.' He dragged in a calming breath to recover his temper.

But it was too late. Hester had already pulled free and that fragile promise was lost.

The photographer quickly retreated to the rear of the plane.

'Everyone will assume this marriage is only because of the coronation requirement.' Her cheeks were still flushed as she sat in the seat and picked up that damn tablet again. He wished he'd never given it to her. 'Do you think it's really necessary for us to try to sell this as a love match?'

'You don't want to be treated as a joke. I have no desire for that either.' Oddly he felt more responsibility about that now. A flicker of protectiveness towards her had surged. 'I think we can pull it off. Who's to say it's not so?'

She hesitated. 'Okay, but the agreement is just between us. Not written down anywhere. I don't want lawyers getting involved and leaking information.'

'You trust that I won't renege on our deal?'

'You have more to lose than I do.' She leaned back into the corner of her chair, still staring at the tablet screen. 'Your reputation actually matters.'

She determinedly studied the information he'd put together for her to do a good job. Yet at the same time, she was determined not to care what anyone thought. Not even him. She seemed to care, yet not.

Intrigued, he studied her. Even in that gorgeous green silk dress, she reminded him of a little sparrow, carefully not taking up too much space in case she was chased away. Only taking crumbs and not demanding anything more. Why was that? Why wasn't she close to her family? Why had she not invited any friends to the wedding? It puzzled him because she was kind. Her friendliness to that feral cat showed that. And more telling, was her relationship with Fi. Fiorella, for all her faults, was a good judge of character. And it wasn't that she hadn't wanted to lose Hester as her assistant. It was that she'd been concerned for her. Was that because Fi saw vulnerability beneath that serenity as well?

The insidious warmth steadily built within him. He could go without intimacy for a year, of *course* he could. But his body rebelled at the thought. He was attracted to her and that attraction seemed to be building by the second. He gritted his teeth, determined to master it, because he was going to have to keep his fiancée close over these next few days and there could be no risk of complicating what should be a perfectly amicable agreement.

'This isn't enough.' She glanced up at him.

'Pardon?'

'I understand more about Triscari's population, economy and geography than I ever thought I'd want to. I know the potted history of your royal family and all that drama with the palace and the castle stuff. But I don't know about *you*.'

A ripple of pleasure skittered down his spine. She was curious about him?

'If I'm to convince people we're a couple then I need to know some facts,' she added primly.

Oh, she just wanted meaningless facts?

'You want my dating profile?' he teased, then chuckled at the glowering look she shot him. 'I enjoy horses, playing polo. My star sign is Scorpio. Apparently that makes me passionate—'

'What are your weaknesses?' she interrupted with a bored tone. 'What do you hate?'

So there *was* a little real curiosity there.

'I hate pickles. And I hate being told what to do.' He stared at her pointedly. 'By anyone.'

She gazed limpidly at him, not backing down. 'What else?'

'You're not taking notes,' he said softly.

'I'm not taking the risk of anyone finding them.'

'Very untrusting, aren't you?'

'Don't worry. I won't forget. *Passionately loathes pickles. And don't tell him what to do,*' she parroted and then shrugged. 'Not so difficult.'

Perversely he decided he wouldn't mind a few commands to fall from her lips. 'Tell me about you. What are your weaknesses?'

Her gaze slid to the side of him. 'I don't have any.'

He chuckled at her flat-out bravado. But it was also a way of keeping him shut out. Ordinarily he didn't mind not getting to know all that much about a woman he was dating, but Hester was going to be his *wife*. And he needed to trust her more than he'd trusted anyone in a long time. Yet she had no hesitation in lying to his face—to protect herself.

'So you expect to learn personal things about me, but won't share any of your own?' He equably pointed out her hypocrisy.

'I've already told you everything personal that's relevant. I told you my parents died when I was a child, that I'm not close to what family I have left, that my life to date has been pretty quiet. There really isn't much else.'

Rigidly determined, wasn't she? That flickering spark within her fired *his* determination. He could quiz her on the meaningless facts too. And he could push for more beyond that. 'Favourite pizza topping?' he prompted.

'Just plain—tomato and cheese.'

'Really? You don't want capers, olives, chilli oil?' He shook his head. 'You're missing out.'

'I don't need a whole bunch of extras.'

'No frills? No added luxuries—just the bare necessities? That's what you'll settle for?' He was stunned and yet when he thought of that dire bedroom of hers, it made sense. 'Tempt your palate a little, Hester. Why not treat yourself to a little something more, or don't you think you deserve it?'

Her jaw dropped. 'It's not about whether I deserve it—'

'Isn't it?' He leaned forward, pleased at her higher pitch. 'Why shouldn't you have all the extras? Other people take them all the time.'

'What if you end up with all the frills and no foundations? Then you discover you've got nothing of substance. Nothing to sustain you.' She put the tablet on the table between them. 'Keeping things simple works for me. The basics suffice.'

The basics? Was that what she considered that soulless cell of a bedroom? But that she didn't even seem to want to *try* something new was interesting. 'Are you afraid to take risks, Hester?'

'Yes,' she said baldly. 'I've fought too long and hard for what I have.'

Her admission surprised him on two counts—

firstly, she didn't seem to *have* all that much. And secondly, she'd taken a massive risk with him and she was nailing this with a stunningly cool ability to adapt and handle all the challenges he was flinging at her. 'Yet you said yes to me—to this impulsive marriage.'

'Because it was an offer too good to pass up.' She gazed at him directly.

'You mean the money. Not the pleasure of my company?'

She blinked rapidly but through those glorious lashes she kept her golden focus on him. 'Yes.'

She sounded breathy and he'd like to think she was lying again because he really didn't think she was the materialistic type. He'd bet even more money that this wasn't about what she could buy but what she could *do*. Was this about freedom— so she didn't have to live on campus any more, helping first-year students get their heads around essay requirements and bibliographic details? Was this because she wanted freedom, not just from work, but from being around other people?

'Well, I'm sorry, Ms Moss, but we're going to have to spend quite a lot of time together over the next few days.' He reached forward, fastened her seat belt for landing and flashed a wicked smile at her. 'I don't know about you, but I can't wait.'

CHAPTER FOUR

TRISCARI SAT LIKE a conglomerate of emeralds and sapphires in the heart of the Mediterranean Sea. As if that giant jeweller in the sky had gathered her most prized stones in the cup of her hand and cast them into the purest blue sea in the most sun-kissed spot on the earth. And in their heart, she'd placed treasure in the form of more valuable minerals. It was incredibly attractive, wealthy and secure.

Hester already knew a lot, having researched it when she first found out she'd been selected as Princess Fiorella's safe college roommate and tutor. But now she'd read more closely about the economic success story and envy of all other small European nations. The royal family had maintained their place on the world stage and now, as ruler of a democracy, the King was mostly a figurehead and facilitator, overseeing the rights of all its people. And promoting it as a destination of course. But that was easy given the world had long been captivated by, not only the kingdom's beauty, but the luxury and the lifestyle it offered. Visiting Triscari topped absolutely everyone's bucket list.

Today the sun peeked above the horizon and turned the sea gold, making the islands look like the literal treasure they were. Hester decided she'd entered a dream world. She'd survived her first ever flight—travelling in pure luxury for hours—to arrive in the most perfect, pristine place in the world.

Ten minutes after the plane had landed, Hester followed Alek down the flight of stairs and onto the tarmac. The air was balmy even this early in the morning—the atmosphere radiated golden warmth. She got into the waiting vehicle and gazed out of the window, hungry to take in more. The stunning scenery suppressed her nerves as the car sped along the street. She knew the palace was in the centre of the town while a cliff-top castle was at the water's edge. The twin royal residences had been constructed for the King and Queen of four hundred years ago. According to the legends, that arranged marriage had spectacularly failed. The couple had determinedly lived separate lives and set up their own rival courts, vying for the title of 'best'. Both had grand halls and opulent gardens and stunning artwork that had been added to over the ages.

'This would have to be the most beautiful

place...' Hester said, her breath taken away by the vista. She glanced at him. 'You must love it.'

'I am very lucky.' His eyes glittered like the night sky. 'I'll do anything for this country.'

'Even get married?'

'Even that.' He nodded. 'Thanks to you.'

'Who'll be meeting us?'

'Senior palace officials.' His expression turned rueful. 'We'll ignore them for the most part, but some things will be unavoidable.'

'You live in the palace?'

'It is where the King resides.' He nodded. 'The Queen's castle is purely for display these days, but the night before the wedding you'll have to stay there. You'll process from there to the palace for the marriage ceremony. People will line the streets to watch. It's the symbolism of unity...no warring with the wife...mainly, it's just tradition.'

The men waiting for them in the vast room were all older than Alek and were all failing to mask their incredibly curious expressions. They watched her approach as if they were judge, jury and executioner in their funereal clothing and they bowed deeply as Alek introduced them.

'Very little is known about Hester and our relationship,' Alek said smoothly. 'I'm aware that where there is a vacuum, the media will fill it with fantasy over fact so we'll fill it. We'll undertake one official appearance to celebrate the engagement. Hester cannot go straight into full-time duties, certainly not right before the wedding. We have a few days but it's not long. She needs time to adjust.'

Hester watched surprise flash over the men's faces.

'Of course, Alek. It is customary for a princess to have attendants to guide her. I thought perhaps—'

'I'll guide her.' Alek cut him off.

'But—'

'We want to be together,' Alek added with a silken smile. 'If we need further support, I'll let you know. I'll meet with you shortly to discuss other issues, but I need to settle Hester into her rooms.'

As the men left Hester turned to face him. 'Do you expect me to speak at this engagement?' The thought terrified her but she was determined to hide that fact. She'd keep calm, carry on.

He glanced at her, amusement flickering in his eyes. 'Only to one person at a time, you won't address a whole room. We will need to do one pre-recorded interview, but I'll be beside you and we'll vet the questions beforehand so you have time to prepare an answer. If you smile, then we'll get through it easily.'

'All I need to do is smile?'

'You have a nice smile.'

'I can do more than smile.'

'Yeah?' His mouth quirked. 'Well, if you could look at me adoringly, that would also help.'

She rolled her eyes.

'And call me Alek.'

'You're quite stuck on that, aren't you?'

'I'm not the one who's stuck.' But his smirk slipped as he sighed. 'I inherited my father's advisors and they're used to things being done a certain way. Change is inevitable, but it's also inevitably slow.'

'Some people find change hard,' she said primly. 'It frightens them.'

'Does it frighten you?' He cocked his head.

'Of course.' She laughed. 'But I'm determined to hide it.'

'Why?' He stepped closer to her. 'You do that a lot, right? Hide your feelings. You do it well.'

'Is that a compliment or a criticism?' she asked lightly.

'Maybe it's just a comment.' His voice dropped to that delicious softness again that implied seductive intimacy—laced with steel.

'With no sentiment behind it?' She shook her head. 'There's always a judgement. That's what people do.'

'True.' He nodded. 'You judged me.'

She stared at him.

'My lifestyle.' He flicked his eyebrows suggestively.

She fought back the flush. 'I never thought you'd be so sensitive to an idle comment.'

'It wasn't idle and you're still judging me right now,' he teased. 'You don't know me, Hester.'

Her heart thudded. 'I know all I need to.'

'A bullet list of preferences that might change in an hour? That's not knowing me.'

'It's just enough detail to give this believability. I don't need to get to know you any more...'

'Intimately?' he suggested in that silken voice. *'Personally?'*

Those dimples were winking at her again. He was so unfairly handsome. And she'd never stood this close to someone in years. Never trusted that someone wouldn't hurt her—with words, or a pinch or a spiteful tug of her hair. So personal space was a thing. Wary, she stepped back, even though there was a large part of her buried deep inside that didn't want her to move in that direction at all.

'I'm going to be your husband,' he pointed out quietly.

'No. You're going to be my boss.'

'Partner.'

'Boss,' she argued. 'You're paying me.'

'You *are* afraid.' He brushed the back of his hand across her jaw ever so lightly. 'Tell me why.'

She froze at his caress, at his scrutiny. She couldn't think how to answer as tension strained between them. She was torn between the desire to flee or fall into his arms. Just as she feared her control would snap, he stepped back.

The dimples broke his solemnity. 'Come on, I have something to show you.'

She traipsed after him along endless corridors with vaulted ceilings and paintings covering every inch of the walls. Even the doors were massive. 'I'm never going to find my way back here. I need breadcrumbs or something.'

He laughed and pushed open yet another door. 'This is your space.'

'My space?'

'Your apartment.'

Her what? She stepped inside and took a second to process the stunningly ornate antechamber.

'It spans two stories within this wing of the palace, but is fully self-contained.' Alek detailed the features. 'You have a lounge, study, small kitchen, bedroom plus a spare, inward-facing balconies for privacy and of course bathroom facilities. You can redecorate it however you wish.'

She couldn't actually get past this initial reception room. 'I have all this to myself?'

'A year is a long time.' Alek circled his hand in the air as he stepped forward. 'I want you to be happy. I want you to feel like it's your home. You can have privacy and space.' He faced her. 'You can build your own library of thrillers in here if you wish.'

Hester stared at the massive room. No one had ever offered her anything like this in her life. When she'd moved to her aunt's house, she'd not been offered the same kind of welcome. And she'd tried *so* hard to fit in. But it had been awkward and they'd made her feel as if it was such a sacrifice to have her take up some of their precious space. She'd felt uncomfortable, unable to change anything for fear of offending them. She'd accumulated nothing much of her very own and that was good, given what had happened. And that minimalist habit had extended to her time at the campus. The rooms were so small, and she'd not cluttered them with anything other than books. So now, confronted with this kind of generosity, emotion choked, not just her throat, but her thinking. It was too much. Everything he'd already done was too much. He'd submerged her in an abundance that she couldn't handle. She gripped her little backpack as her limbs trembled. Frozen and tongue-tied, she couldn't trust herself to move.

'They've brought your suitcase in already,' he said.

She saw it next to one of the enormous comfortable-looking armchairs. She had such little stuff for such an opulent space it was ridiculous.

His eyebrows pulled together and he hesitated a moment before stepping towards the window. 'There's good views across to the ocean and the balcony in your bedroom is completely private. No one will be able to see you.' He paused again and she felt him gazing at her. 'Do you not like it?'

'No.' She could hardy speak for the emotion completely clogging her up. She stared hard at the floor, knowing that if she blinked some of that hot, burning liquid was going to leak from her eyes and she really didn't want that to happen. Then she realised she'd said the wrong thing. 'Not no. I meant... I just...it's fine.'

'Fine,' he echoed, but his voice sounded odd. 'So why do you look like...?' He trailed off and stepped closer than before and there was nothing for her to hide behind. 'You look like you're about to cry.'

She felt that wall of awkwardness rise and slick mortification spread at the realisation he could read her all too easily. Why could she suddenly not hide her feelings? And worse, why couldn't she hold them back?

'I don't cry.' It wasn't a lie—until now.

'Not ever—?'

'Do you?' she interrupted him, forcing herself to swallow back the tears and throw him off guard the way he was her.

He gazed at her intently and it was even worse. 'Hester—'

'I'm *fine.*' She dragged in a breath, but couldn't pull it together enough to keep it all back. 'It's just that I've never had such a big place all to myself.'

The confession slithered out, something she'd never trusted anyone enough to tell before. She didn't want him to think she didn't appreciate the effort he'd gone to. She knew he had insane wealth and property, but he'd thought this through for her. He'd taken time to consider what she might like. No one had done that for her. Not since she'd lost her parents. So she deeply appreciated this gesture, but she really needed to hold herself together because she couldn't bear to unravel completely before him.

She sensed him remain near her for a strained moment but then he strolled back towards the window.

'Personally I think the wallpaper in here is a bit much.' He casually nodded at the ferociously ornate green and black pattern.

Startled, she glanced across at him.

'You have to agree,' he added drolly. 'The word would be gaudy.'

She couldn't contain the giggle that bubbled up, a fountain of pure silliness. As her face creased, that tear teetered over the edge and she quickly wiped its trail from her cheek.

'I'm right, aren't I?' If he'd noticed her action, he didn't comment. Instead he wriggled his finger at the seam where wallpaper met window frame until he tugged enough loose to tear it.

'Alek!'

'Oh, the press are going to love it if you say my name with that hint of censure,' he teased in an altogether different tone.

A shock wave of heat blasted through her. Its impact was explosive, ripping through her walls to release the raw awareness. She'd been determined to ignore it. She knew he was an outrageous flirt, but it wasn't his tone or his teasing jokes that caused this reaction within her. It was *everything* about him. He made her wonder about the kind of intimacy she'd never known. The kind she'd actively avoided. And she'd never wanted to step *closer* to a person before.

'Don't be afraid to ask for what you want, Hester,' he said softly.

She stared at him blankly, her mind going in all kinds of searing directions.

'You can do what you like,' he offered. 'Take out walls, rip up the carpet, whatever.'

Oh. Right. He meant the rooms. Only she hadn't been thinking about the décor and what she feared she *wanted* was far too forbidden.

'Don't worry about the budget. I can just sell one of my horses to cover it.'

'Don't you love your horses more than anything?' She tried to break her unfortunate fixation.

'Other than my crown and my sister?' he teased. 'Or my playboy lifestyle?'

She licked her dried lips and refused to continue along that track. 'Do you have an apartment in here too?'

'Right next door.' He nodded. 'It's best if we're near each other.'

'I understand, it needs to look okay.' She made herself agree. 'Because this is a job,' she reiterated. But it was a lie already. 'It's just an act.'

With no intimacy—emotional or otherwise.

His gaze narrowed. 'I'd like to think we can be friends, Hester.'

She didn't have friends. Acquaintances and colleagues, yes. But not friends. Since the rejection she'd suffered after her parents' deaths, she'd not been able to trust people, not got to know anyone well. Not even Princess Fiorella.

But she sensed that Alek expected a little more from her and perhaps that was fair enough. It wasn't right for her to judge him based on the actions of others he didn't even know. Or on the salacious reports the media wrote about him. She had to take him on his own actions around her and so far she had to admit he'd been decent. He'd done everything in his power to make this as easy as possible for her. And it wasn't his fault she was attracted to him like *that*. That element was up to her to control.

'I'm sure we can.' But inwardly she froze, petrified by her own internal reaction to him.

Her brain was fixed along one utterly inappropriate track. She had the horrible feeling it was like the teen girl's first crush she'd never actually had. The fact was he didn't need to do or say anything but he'd half seduced her already. Could she really be so shallow as to be beguiled by his looks alone?

'It's going to be fine,' she said firmly. 'We have a whole year and most of the time I'll stay safe inside the palace, right?' She moved into the room, faking her comfort within the large, luxurious space. 'Actually I'm happy to stay here while you go to that meeting now, if you like.'

His eyes widened. 'Are you dismissing me, Hester?'

She smiled at his mild affront. 'Are you not used to that?'

'You know I'm not.'

'You'll get used to it.' She couldn't help a small giggle as she echoed his own reassurance.

'What if I don't want to?' He stepped closer.

Hester swallowed her smile and stilled. For a

long moment they just stared at each other. Then, once more, he took a step back and the dimples flickered ever so briefly.

'I'm afraid I need you for another few minutes to show you something else.' He gestured towards the door.

'Do I need string?' She grimaced.

He chuckled. 'It's very near.'

She followed him through another doorway and then down a curling flight of stairs and blinked on the threshold of a huge airy space. There was a gorgeous pool—half indoor, half out, surrounded by lush plantings and private sun loungers.

'My father had this built for Fiorella's privacy, but she wanted her freedom. After my mother died, my father became overprotective and the palace became a bit of a prison for her.'

Hester swallowed at the mention of his mother. She'd not been brave enough to ask him about her at all. 'Was it a prison for you too?'

'I was older. And—as bad as it sounds—I was a guy. He didn't have the same concerns for me as he did for her.'

'Seriously?'

'I know,' he sighed. 'Double standards suck. She was a lot younger though and she'd lost her mother. Everyone needs some freedom of choice, don't they? Fi definitely did.'

'She told me you helped her get your father's approval for her to study abroad,' Hester said. 'That it was only because you promised to stay and do all the royal duties that she could go. And that now your father's gone, you've told her she can do whatever she wants.'

He glanced out across the water. 'She enjoys her studies. She should have the freedom and opportunity to finish them. She's a smart woman.'

Hester's curiosity flared. 'What would you have done if you'd had the same freedom of choice that Fiorella now does?'

His smile was distant. 'There was never that choice for me, Hester.'

Alek's phone buzzed and he quickly checked the message. 'The wedding dress designers have arrived.'

Oh. She'd forgotten about that. But she found herself anticipating the planning—she'd very recently decided that there was something to be said for smoke and mirrors. The look on his face when she'd appeared after her airplane make-over had been both reward and insult. She'd quite like to surprise him some more.

'Is there a particular style you'd like for my dress?' she asked demurely.

He gazed at her for a moment, his eyes narrowing. 'I'm sure you'll look amazing in whatever you choose to wear.' But his dimples suddenly appeared. 'Though I do wonder if you'll dare to go beyond the basics for once.'

'Feathers and frills?'

'Why not?' He led her back to her apartment where Hester found the women waiting. Hester drew in a deep breath and followed them in.

Four hours later Alek was hot and tired from going through the military-like wedding arrangements with his advisors and answering all their incessant questions. The media had already begun staking out the palace. The news had reverberated in a shock wave around the world. The news channels were running nothing but the photo that had been taken in the plane on the way over and digging deep for nuggets about Hester already. Fortunately her family were already on their way over and unable to comment because he'd ensured Wi-Fi wasn't available on their flight so he still had time to guide their speculation.

Though he'd learned more about her in the small pieces being published as soon as they were written than from her own too-brief mentions of her past. The bald facts were there, but the real truth of her? The depth? He doubted the investigative reporters would get anywhere near it. She was so self-contained even he was struggling and he was the one *with* her. What had happened to her parents? Why was she so alone? What did she keep in that broken little box that she kept nearby at all times?

'Alek?'

He blinked, recalling his concentration. He couldn't waste time wondering what made her tick—what secrets and hurts she held close—he had to run the palace, reply to invitations to tour another country, clarify Triscari's position on a new European environmental accord, and not least decide the next steps for the stud programme at his stables. Too much at the best of times.

Yet he still couldn't help thinking about Hester, concerned about how she was dealing with all those designers and the decisions she had to make, wondering how else he could make her comfortable. He'd liked being able to do something that had truly moved her—seeing her real response pierce her calm exterior had been oddly exhilarating. He wanted to mine more of that deeply buried truth from her and know for sure he'd pleased her.

In the end he called an assistant to check on his fiancée's movements and report back. Five minutes later he learned she'd been cloistered in her rooms this whole time. Stifling a grimace, Alek turned back to the paperwork spread on the vast table before him. The prospect of their impending marriage strangled him, fogging his usual sharp decision-making ability, making everything take longer. Another hour passed and he was almost at the point of bursting in on Hester himself, just to ensure they hadn't accidentally suffocated her in all that silk.

'Enough.' He pushed back when his advisors raised another thorny problem.

He'd been issuing instructions for hours and he was done.

If it were an ordinary day, he'd go for a ride to clear his head. But today wasn't anything like ordinary and he couldn't leave the confines of the palace, what with all the media gulls gathering. Irritated with being even more tightly constrained than usual, he impatiently stalked towards his wing. The tug deep inside drawing him there was desperation for his own space, wasn't it? It wasn't any need to see her.

He gritted his teeth as he reached her door and pushed himself past it. But once he was in his own room he heard soft splashes through the open window. He paused. Was someone in the pool?

He swiftly glanced out of the window. The view all but killed his brain as his blood surged south. Those utility trousers and tee had done a good job of hiding her figure. So had those two dresses, even, with their floaty fabric and draping styles. Because now, in that plain, black, purely functional swimsuit, Hester Moss was even more lush in particular parts than he'd expected. She truly was a goddess. And maybe this marriage wasn't going to be as awful as he'd imagined. Already teasing her was a delight, while touching her a temptation he was barely resisting.

For the first time in his life he was pleased his father had been so overprotective towards his sister. That he'd ensured the pool was completely secure from prying eyes—beyond these private apartments, of course. In fact, the whole palace was a fortress. No one could see in and, with the air restrictions in place, no helicopters could fly over with cameras on board. He opened the door to his balcony and lightly ran down the curling stone steps to the private courtyard.

She was swimming lazy lengths and apparently hadn't noticed his arrival. It wasn't until she rolled onto her back that she saw him. Her eyes widened and she sank like a stone beneath the surface before emerging again with a splutter. He was so tempted to skim his hands over her creamy skin and sensual curves. He ached to test their silkiness and softness for himself. Except she now hid—ducking down in the blue so only her head poked above the gentle ripples she'd caused.

'What are you doing?' Her gold eyes were huge.

Uninhibited—and frankly exhilarated—he'd undone his shirt buttons before he'd even thought about it. Now he laughed at the look on her face. 'Relax. It's just skin. And it's a pool.'

'You can't swim naked,' she said, scandalised.

'I told you, the pool is completely private. No one can see us—it's designed so only our private apartments overlook it. Mine, yours, Fi's. And Fi isn't here.'

'You still can't swim naked,' she choked.

'Relax, Hester.' He laughed, amused by her blushing outrage.

'You just do everything you want, don't you?'

'Not all the time. Not everything.'

She had no idea how well behaved he was being right now. Another bolt of attraction seared through him. He kept his black knit boxers on but swiftly dived into the pool to hide the very direct effect she was having on him.

'How'd the fitting go?' he asked once he swam to the surface again. The thought of her in a fancy wedding dress intrigued him. The dresses on the plane had been stunning, but some white lacy bridal thing? He suspected she'd slay it.

'It was fine.'

Of course she'd say that—it was her fall-back phrase to conceal every real thought and emotion. He gazed into her eyes, wishing he could read her mind. Only the softest signs gave her away—her pupils had swollen so there was only a slight ring of colour visible; her cheeks had reddened slightly; her breath sounded a little fast and shallow. But he wanted to provoke a *real* reaction from her—powerful, visceral, *uncontrollable*.

'Alek?' she asked.

Despite the uncertainty in her tone, primal satisfaction scoured his insides, tightening every muscle with anticipation. He really did like his name on her lips. That small success would be the first of many. And he understood the reason for her uncertainty and slight breathlessness. She had a similar effect on him.

He swam closer, hiding his straining body beneath the cool water. Her eyelashes were so amazing—droplets glistened on the ends of a few, enhancing their lushness even more and framing her jewel-like irises to mesmerising perfection. She was every inch a luscious lioness.

'What are you doing?' she muttered as he floated closer still.

'Tell me how the fitting went,' he said softly. 'Tell me something more than a mere platitude.'

'Why?'

'Because I want to know how you're feeling.'

That wary look entered her eyes, but at the same time the water's warmth rose a notch. The tension between them was now half exposed and she couldn't tear her gaze from him any more than he could peel his from her.

'Why?' Her lips parted in a tempting pout—ruby red berries promising delectable, juicy softness.

'Because we're going to be a team, Hester,' he muttered, struggling to focus and to keep his hands off her. 'I'd like to know how you're feeling, how you're coping with everything. We should be able to communicate openly with each other.' He cocked his head. 'I get that you're quite self-contained, but this doesn't need to be difficult.'

Except it felt complicated. Something drew him closer even when he shouldn't. This should be straightforward. Where had this vast curiosity come from? Or this gnawing desire that now rippled through every cell in his body? It hadn't been there yesterday when he'd proposed. But now? Now he wanted to *know* her—and not just in that biblical sense. He wanted to understand what she was thinking and why. Drawing her out was a challenge. It wasn't unlike detangling Fi's glass Christmas tree lights for her when he was younger—careful focus, gentle hands and infinite patience were required.

But Alek wasn't feeling brilliantly patient this second. His heart was thudding too fast. He couldn't resist reaching out to feel for himself how soft she was, placing his hands on her slender waist and pulling her closer to where he stood.

Hester braced her hands on his broad forearms,

feeling the strength of his muscles beneath her palms. Her pulse quickened and, despite the cool water, her temperature soared.

'Have you decided to seduce me?' Her voice was the barest thread of a whisper.

He gazed at her intently but said nothing.

Old fears slithered in, feeding doubt and fattening the insecurity that he could never possibly *mean* it. This was just a game for him. He was so used to winning, wasn't he?

'What are you going to do once you've succeeded?' She couldn't hold back the note of bitterness. 'Discard me like disposable cutlery?'

He didn't flinch at her lame dig. His gaze was unwavering and she was drowning in the depths of darkness in his eyes. 'Are you saying I'm going to succeed?'

'A man with your experience is always going to succeed against someone like me.'

He gazed at her relentlessly and something dangerous flickered from him to her. 'You're really not experienced?'

'Of course not,' she snapped as the unfamiliar tension in her body pushed her towards rejection—it was that or something so reckless. So impossible. She'd all but told him back in Boston. 'In your impossible quest for an appropriate bride you've found a virgin fit for a king.' The bitter irony rose within her.

His hands tightened on her waist. 'You're a *virgin*?'

What else did 'not experienced' mean?

'Don't act like you didn't guess already,' she angrily snapped.

'How? And why would I?' He shook her gently. 'You said you'd had a quiet life, but this is…'

'Irrelevant,' she slammed back at him. 'We have an agreement. You're paying me to do a job. Physical intimacy, other than those two kisses, is off the table.'

But she was finding it impossible to breathe, impossible to tear her gaze from his. And it was impossible to do this 'job' when he kept stripping off and smiling at her all the time.

'Is it, Hester?' he breathed.

Why did he have to be so beautiful? Why did her body have to choose this moment to spark to life and decide it wanted touch? The sort of touch she'd never craved before. Not like this—not with a bone-deep driving need that was almost impossible to restrain.

'Please let me go.' And the worst thing happened—because it wasn't the assertive command she wanted. It was a breathless plea, totally undermined by the thread of desire that was so obvious to her that she knew it was evident to him as well.

But he didn't release her.

'Just so you know, sweetheart, it will not be my "experience" that sees me succeed with you,' he said firmly and then swept her up to sit her on the side of the pool. 'It's not *me* at all.'

He pushed back, floating away from her, leaving her with a parting shot so powerful she was glad she wasn't still standing.

'It'll happen only when *you* decide that I'm the one you want.' He levered up out of the pool on the opposite side and she watched him stride away in all his sopping, masculine beauty. 'You're the one with the power. You're the one who will need to say yes.'

CHAPTER FIVE

HESTER GRIPPED HER new clutch purse tightly. Her dress was suitable, she could walk in her mid-heeled nude shoes, and she'd practised not blinking so she could cope with banks of cameras… it was going to be fine. It was one sequence of appearances on one day—TV interview, public outing and back to the palace. She could manage that. She'd been practising often enough. The last few days had whizzed by in a flurry of meetings and planning. Alek had been with her much of the time but he was constantly interrupted and often completely called away. But she'd hidden in the palace, preparing for the performance of a lifetime, practising the walk down the long aisle of the chapel, climbing into the carriage, then swimming in the pool each afternoon. But he'd not joined her there again.

Now he was already waiting in the corridor. As always her tummy flipped when she saw him, but it was the burn building *below* her belly—that restless, hot ache—that was the real problem. She couldn't look at him without that appalling temptation to slide closer, to soften completely and let him touch… She still couldn't believe she'd made that embarrassing confession the other day. Her virginal status had surprised him and he hadn't denied he was interested in her physically. But he could have any woman he wanted. So she needed to forget all that and remember that this was a *job*.

His appraisal of her was uncharacteristically serious—all jet-black eyes, square jaw and no dimples. She sensed his leashed power; after all, he was a man who could move mountains with the snap of his fingers.

'Your hair's down.' He finally spoke. 'I like it.'

'I'm so glad to hear that,' she muttered, letting her tension seep out with uncharacteristic acidity. 'All I ever wanted was your approval.'

'Excellent.' He smiled wolfishly, soaking up her faux sweetness and ignoring the blatant sarcasm. 'You have it. I knew you'd deliver.'

Gritting her teeth, she wished she wouldn't react to his low chuckle but warmth pooled deep inside regardless. She liked it when he teased her with this sparkle-tipped talk that turned tension into bubbling moments of fun. The kind she'd never had with anyone before.

'Ready to hold hands?' He tilted his chin at her, his eyes gleaming with challenge.

'To stop me running away?' she cooed, then snapped on some seriousness. 'Good idea.'

He took her hand in a firm grip and led her into a vast room filled with fascinating sculptures and books. She could lose herself happily in here for days but she barely had time to blink at all the gold-framed art on the walls because he swiftly guided her to a lamp-lit polished wooden desk. 'Come on, you need to choose something.'

She gaped at the velvet-lined display cases carefully placed on the table before glancing up to see a liveried man with white kid gloves discreetly leaving the room.

'Wow, you've presented so many options...' She didn't quite know what to say. There were dozens of stunning rings—diamond solitaires, sapphire clusters, ruby squares and others she had no idea of.

'I'm hoping one will fit.' Alek's brows drew together as he looked down at her. 'You have small hands.'

'Did you raid all the jewellery shops in a thousand-mile radius?'

'No, these are from the palace vault.' He smiled at her horrified expression. 'There are a number of things in there. You'll choose a tiara for the wedding later this afternoon. We don't have time for that right now and it's supposed to be a secret from me, I think.'

There was a whole vault full of priceless treasure? She stared brainlessly at the tray, stunned yet again by the extreme wealth of his lifestyle—and of his ancient heritage, steeped in tradition. As impossible to believe as it was, she knew all those gleaming stones were real. Just as their impending marriage was real.

'Which do you like?' he prompted.

She shook her head, dazed. 'Any of them. They're all amazing.'

And it was impossible to decide. Still silence followed her comment, but she was frozen with fear and awe and stinging embarrassment.

'Would you like me to help?'

She heard the smile in his voice but she couldn't smile back. 'You can just choose.'

'You should have something you actually like,' he said dryly and then lowered his voice. 'You *deserve* something you like, Hester.' He turned her to face him, making her look up to meet his gaze. 'There's no wrong answer here. You can pick whichever you want...'

It was very kind of him, but way too overwhelming. Pearls, diamonds, emeralds, sapphires, rubies...she was stunned and speechless and so deeply discomfited by his careful concern. It made it worse somehow—that he knew she wasn't used to people consulting her on what she would like, or giving her beautiful rooms to sleep in, or choices of sublime designer gowns and now priceless, beautifully crafted jewels.

'Why don't you start by trying some on to see if they even fit?' He plucked the nearest ring from the tray and grasped her cold hand.

Hester remained motionless as he slid the ring down her finger before removing it again and selecting another with rapid decisiveness. The enormous oval emerald was too enormous. The square ruby's band was too big... As he tested and discarded several options, he kept a firm grip on her hand as if he thought she really might run away if he didn't. Maybe she would've too, because her core temperature was rising and her breathing shortening. He was too near and she was too tense. She just wanted one to fit well enough so this could be done and she could get away from him.

'This makes you feel awkward, Hester?' he murmured, glancing up into her eyes.

Yes, because he was standing so close and it felt too intimate, not the businesslike process it ought to be. Her imagination was working overtime, reading too much into every look, every word—that he was subtly teasing her by lingering as if he knew how much his proximity affected her and he was playing on it.

'Of course it does.' She tried to match his careless confidence but her voice wouldn't get above a whisper. She fell back on practicalities to answer half honestly. 'I'm going to be too scared to go anywhere with something like this on my finger. What if I lose it?'

'You only need to wear it to the events today and the wedding ceremony. The rest of the time, it'll remain safe in the vault.'

Okay. Good. That made it a little better. So she nodded and held still as he tried another that had a too-large band.

'You don't have a favourite colour?' he asked as he cocked his head to study how the next option looked on her small hand.

She shook her head, too embarrassed to articulate anything. It was impossible to think when he was this near to her and holding her with firm gentleness.

'Okay, then I'm going to decide,' he said. 'And you're not getting any say.'

She would've laughed if she weren't so flummoxed by his intense effect on her. With exaggerated movements he angled his body to hide her own hand from her. She felt the sensuous slide of his fingers down hers as he tried a few more rings. But his broad shoulders and masculine body blocked her view. Then he slowed, trying one, then another—then another and taking far longer with one. All the while she stared at the fine stitching on the seam of his jacket.

He turned his head to glance at her, a smile flitting around his lips in a mysterious way. 'I'm done.'

With a flourish, he pivoted to face her, sliding his hold to the tips of her fingers so she could see the ring he'd placed on her.

'What do you think?' he gently prompted.

She just stared. But inside while her heart pounded, her brain was starved of anything useful. It was stunning. One she'd been unable to see at first glance because she'd been blinded by so many gleaming options. It was a fine gold band and a solitary diamond. But the massive stone was cut into a teardrop shape—it didn't glitter brilliantly, wasn't gaudy, but rather the multifaceted cut ensured it gleamed and gave it a depth she'd not thought possible from a mere mineral. She could get lost looking into it. It was exquisite and delicate and moved her unbearably.

'Hester?'

Unable to resist responding to that commanding thread in his voice, she glanced up. Her tongue was cleaved to the roof of her mouth. Her pulse thudded through her body with such ferocity she had to stay completely still to control it—to stop that overwhelming emotion exploding out of her in an ugly mess. It was too risky to reveal anything vulnerable—that something might *matter* to her. But the warmth in the backs of Alek's eyes was different now. There wasn't only that flicker of flirtation and teasing awareness. There was something deeper than both those things and as the seconds passed in silence it only strengthened.

'It's fine,' she croaked.

She knew her response was so woefully inadequate it was almost rude, but no way could she utter the incoherent, incomplete thoughts battling in her head amongst the swirl of confusion. She expected him to either frown or tease, but he didn't. His face lit up and he smiled. Her heart stopped. Those dimples were going to be the death of her.

'Yes, it is.' He curled his arm around her waist and walked her towards the big heavy doors at the other end of the room. 'I'm glad you like it.'

Like it? Total understatement. She couldn't help sneaking peeks at it as she walked with him into a reception room that had been prepared for the interview, but she still couldn't verbalise the hot mess of feeling inside.

The journalist was waiting with only two crew—one for camera, one for sound. Hester perched on the edge of the sofa and hoped her nerves didn't show too much. Alek kept one arm around her and drew her closer to his side while holding her hand throughout. She was so aware of his heat and strength and his smile melted everything and everyone else away until somehow it was over and he was laughing and releasing her only to shake hands with the presenter.

'You did well,' Alek said as he escorted her through the palace maze back to her apartment.

Hester couldn't actually remember a word she'd said in response to the questions, she'd been too aware of him and the slippery direction of her private thoughts. 'Oh, yes, I was amazing. I don't think I said more than three words.'

'Are you fishing for compliments? That wasn't enough for you?' He whirled to face her. 'Ask me for more.' He dared her up close. 'You have no idea how much I want you to ask me for more.' His smile deepened as she gaped at him. 'Oh, you've gone silent again.'

'Because you're a tease.'

'Yeah? Perhaps. But that doesn't mean I don't mean it.' His hand tightened around her wrist. 'Your pulse is quickening.'

'It's terror,' she muttered.

'Liar.' He grinned.

'You're so conceited.'

'Maybe because you've mastered the art of looking at me so adoringly...' He chuckled as she flicked her wrist free of his hold.

'Don't we have to go on this visit now?' She pushed herself back into work mode.

'In an hour, yes.' He leaned closer. 'That's just enough time for—'

'Me to get changed, that's right.' She all but ran back to her apartment to where her stylists were waiting.

'You're nervous?' Alek glanced at her keenly as the car drove them out of the palace gates and through the banks and banks of cameras just over an hour later.

'Is it really obvious?' She worried even more and clutched her bag strap tightly.

'Honestly, I imagine everyone would expect you to be nervous and it's not a bad thing. People like to see the humanity in others.' He reached for her hand and shot her that charming smile.

'They forgive you your sins?' She tried to answer lightly, but beneath it she was glad of the way he rubbed his thumb back and forth over her tense fingers. It was soothing, like when she counted her breathing. But better.

But bad too. Because she didn't want him to stop.

'Nerves aren't a sin.' He laughed. 'They're normal. Everyone has them.'

'Even you?'

'Even me.' He gave an exaggerated nod. 'Does it surprise you that I might feel normal things, Hester?'

That sense of danger as those undercurrents of heat and temptation swirled too close to the surface.

'So this is the paediatric ward visit,' she confirmed needlessly. Just to remember the *job*. Just to stop staring at him. Since when was she so seduced by physical beauty? She'd always tried not to judge people based on their appearance—she knew how it felt to be bullied about things.

'You don't think it's cynical to use sick children to sell us as a couple?' she asked.

'I think that most of these little guys have a really rough road ahead of them, so why shouldn't they get a little joy out of this? I'd far rather spend an hour with them than with some of the captains of industry who don't think I can live up to my father's legacy.'

'You think people don't take you seriously?'

'I'm just the Playboy Prince, aren't I?'

'Wow, I wonder why they have reason to think that?'

'I know, right?' He sent her a mocking look. 'If only they knew I now have a pure and innocent bride to mend me of my disreputable ways...'

'Very funny.'

Except she was revising her opinion on his reputation. It hadn't taken long to see that Alek considered his country and his people in almost every decision he made.

It seemed there were thousands waiting behind police-guarded barriers and every one held a camera or phone up. As she passed them she was terribly glad of her long dress and the firmness with which her hair was pinned. Alek released her hand so they could engage with the people in the receiving line and she received a small bouquet from a sweet young girl. She heard a child bellowing and glanced quickly to see a small boy being carried away by a nurse but she maintained her smile and pretended she hadn't noticed. There was no need to draw attention to someone else's sensory overload.

Alek compelled attention like a black hole, sucking everyone, everything—all the light— into his vortex and onwards he spun, ever more powerful. But she also felt the people watching her, assessing, judging—she could only hope she passed. After a tour of the ward, they spent some time in the hospital classroom where a few children sat at tables working on drawings. At a table near the back, she could see the small boy who'd been hurried away at their arrival. With the 'freedom' to walk around, Hester gravitated towards where he was, subdued and firmly under the control of the teacher standing beside him. Belligerent sadness dimmed his eyes. Hester didn't make eye contact with the teacher, she just took the empty chair at his table. She drew a piece of paper towards her and selected a pencil to colour in with. The boy paused his own colouring to watch her work then resumed his until they reached for the same emerald pencil.

'I think it's a really nice colour,' she said softly, encouraging the boy to take it.

'It's my favourite,' he muttered.

'Mine too,' she whispered with a conspiratorial smile. 'But don't tell anyone.'

She glanced up and encountered Alek's inscrutable gaze. She'd not realised he was nearby.

'Time for us to leave, Hester,' he bent and said quietly. 'But we'll come back again.'

As they were driven back to the palace he turned in his seat to study her face. She was sure it was only for all those cameras along the route.

'You did very well. Again,' he said.

She inclined her head with exaggerated regal poise to accept the compliment.

He suddenly laughed and picked up her hand, playing with the ring on her finger in an intolerably sweet gesture. 'I mean it. Being able to make someone smile or respond—to make a connection like with that boy who'd been distressed?' Alek nodded. 'That was skilled.'

'Not *skilled*.' Hester shook her head. 'I had no clue. I just tried to give him the time to let him get himself together.'

'Natural kindness, then.' Alek ignored the photographers calling outside the car as it slowly cruised through the crowd. 'You told him your favourite colour. Or was that just a lie to make him feel good?'

She paused. 'It was the truth.'

'So you could tell him something you couldn't tell me?'

She paused, startled by the soft bite in that query. 'Have I hurt your feelings?' She tried to deflect him with a smile.

'Yes.'

She shot him a worried glance. Surely he was joking? He intently watched her—not smiling, not glowering either.

'I just wanted to be kind to him.' She drew in a breath. 'Some people get all the attention, right? The loud ones, or the ones confident enough to smile and call out, and the ones who have the tantrums like him. The ones I feel bad for are the quiet ones—who don't push forward or act out, who are so busy being good or polite or scared... sometimes they need to know someone has seen them and I didn't today.'

'I did,' he said softly. 'I went around and saw some of those ones.'

Of course he had—because he'd been doing it all his life. Sharing his attention.

'Were you one of those kids?' he asked. 'One who was being so good she became invisible?'

'Good but not good enough?' She wouldn't have minded being that kid. 'No, that wasn't me.'

'I can't see you confidently calling out things in front of everyone.'

'No, not that one either.'

'Tantrums?' He lifted an eyebrow and sent her a sideways smile. 'No? But what else is there?'

In the safety of the car, riding on the success of her morning and the fact the worst of today was now over, she was relaxed enough actually to answer. 'I was the kid who ran away.'

He watched her. 'You really mean it.'

'I really do.' She drew in a slightly jagged breath, regretting the confession.

'Did they find you and bring you home again?'

'They had to,' she replied lowly. 'I was young and they had an image to maintain. But that didn't stop me trying again.'

'Did you ever succeed in running away for good?'

'Eventually, yes.'

She wanted to gaze out of the window. She wanted to end this conversation. But his coal-black eyes were so full of questions that she couldn't answer and so full of compassion that she didn't have the strength to pull back from him either.

'Will you run away if you don't like it here?' he asked.

'No. I'm grown up now and I'll see this

through.' She made herself smile and clear the intensity. 'I think it's more likely that you'll banish me like your ancestor did his rebel Queen.'

To her relief, he followed her lead and laughed. 'I have to banish you to her castle. I'll take you after dinner. It'll be a dark-windowed car tonight. Tomorrow is the glass carriage.'

'The fairy-tale element?'

'Absolutely.'

After another dinner devoted to preparation and planning, this time with several advisors attending and in which Alek refused to release her hand, they were driven to the castle on the edge of the city for Hester's final night as a single woman.

'Welcome to Queen Aleksandrina's home.' Alek spread his arms wide as the enormous wooden doors were closed behind them.

Hester knew the story of Aleksandrina well. Her marriage had taken place after the King's coronation and was such an unmitigated disaster that a law had been passed stipulating that any future prince could not claim the King's throne before being married. Furthermore, at the King's coronation, his bride must bow before him—before all his other subjects did; she was to be prime symbol of deference to his rule. It was appalling, but 'tradition'.

'The rebel Queen who defied her husband and

decided to build her own castle at the other end of town?' Hester nodded in approval. 'She sounds *amazing*.'

Alek grinned. 'You know I'm named after her?'

'Really?' That surprised her. She'd thought the rebel Queen was frowned upon. 'And you don't want to live here?'

She hoisted her little backpack on her shoulder and gazed up in awe at the carved constellations in the vaulted ceiling of the castle's great room. Where the palace was gilded and gleaming, the castle was hand-carved curves and lush plantings. It was softer somehow and very feminine. Carved into the coastline, it had a wild element to it; part of it actually overhung a cliff.

'There's a tunnel to the beach below. I'll show you.' He grinned at her. 'The rumour was it was how the Queen smuggled her lovers in without the King knowing.'

'Lovers—plural?'

'Apparently she was insatiable.'

'And did you say you're named after her?' Hester clarified a little too meekly.

He chuckled. 'My mother always said those rumours were just slut-shaming to steal her powerful legacy from her. The fact was she was a better queen than he was a king and he couldn't handle it.'

Hester stilled at the mention of his mother. She

sensed she was an off-limits subject and Hester of all people understood the desire to protect those precious memories. 'It sounds like your mother was quite a woman too,' she said lightly.

'She was.' He turned and headed towards a doorway. 'Come to the ballroom.'

Yes, he wasn't about to elaborate and Hester didn't blame him. 'This isn't the ballroom?'

Two minutes later Hester gazed around the vast, ornate room, uttered moved by gorgeous wooden carvings and low-hanging candelabra. 'I…wow… I just…' She trailed off; her throat was too tight. It was so incredible.

Alek stepped in front of her and brushed her cheek with his hand as he gazed into her eyes. 'You really do struggle to express yourself sometimes, don't you?'

Of course, he saw that. Somehow he was right there, too close. Making her want…too much. Everything she *felt* around him was too strong and so easily he weakened the bonds with which she held herself together.

His hand on her waist was so light, so gentle, she couldn't quite be sure it was even there. But the electricity racing along her veins confirmed it. 'What are—?'

'Practising for our first dance,' he answered before she'd even finished asking.

'You're kidding—we have to dance?' She groaned. 'I can't dance, Alek. I don't know how to.'

'Just relax and follow my lead.' His dimples appeared. 'It'll be fine.'

She put her hand on his chest, keeping him at that distance as he stepped fractionally closer. But the tips of her fingers burned with the temptation to spread, to stroke. And they weren't dancing at all, they were standing still as still, close but not breathing, not blinking either. Somehow time evaporated. Somehow he was nearer still and she'd got lost in the depths of his dark eyes and the current of his energy coiling around her.

'Why try to fight it?' he whispered.

Of course he knew, of course he saw the terrible yearning within her. But self-preservation made her deny it. 'Fight what?'

'The inevitable.'

'I refuse to be inevitable,' she muttered hoarsely, her instinctive self-preservation instincts kicking in.

'There's a saying for that,' he countered with a smile. 'Cutting off your nose to spite your face.'

'You think I'm missing out on something amazing just because I won't fall for your flirting?'

'I think it's interesting that you're making it such a big deal.'

'Maybe I want something meaningful.'

'You think I don't mean it?' A frown entered

his eyes. 'Because I do. There's something about you…you're growing on me, Hester.'

'Like a kind of bacteria? Fungus?'

'Not fungus.' Beneath her fingertips she felt the laughter rumble in his broad chest. 'Are you trying to put me off?'

'You know I am.'

'I do.' He shot her a look. 'And I love that you feel the need to try so hard. It makes me think I'm getting beneath that prickly shell of yours.'

'So now I'm a porcupine? And here I was thinking you were supposed to be impossibly charming and irresistible.'

'You know what I think? I think you've decided I'm some big, bad philanderer. And that makes me terrible, for some reason. Sorry for liking sex, sweetheart. Maybe if you tried it, you'd discover it's not so awful. But instead you feel you have to keep me at a distance and not explore the fact that we have quite spectacular chemistry.' He leaned closer. 'Sparks, Hester. Every time we touch. Every time we even see each other.'

She ducked her gaze. 'I just don't think it's wise for us to blur the boundaries. We have a *contract*. That's all.'

'A contract that contains two kisses.' He smiled happily.

Something swooped low in her belly. 'Only two.' And they were both going to be in public so it wasn't as if they were going to develop into anything out of control.

'But you're a lot more fun to be around than I imagined you'd be, Hester.'

'I'm so glad, given I live to please you, my lord.'

He laughed and lightly tapped her on the nose. 'Call me Alek.' He leaned closer and breathed, 'Always.'

Her smile faded. She wished he wouldn't get like this—the combination of playful and serious that was so seductive it shut down her brain and made those dormant secret parts of her roar to life.

'I...don't—' She broke off as a shiver ran down her spine. She stepped back, seeking distance from his intensity.

He stayed where he was, studying her intently. 'Are you afraid of me?'

'Surprisingly, no.' She was too shaken to lie. She didn't fear him so much as how she *felt* when he was near.

'So you're worried about...?' A frown knitted his brows.

It was easier to talk about everything else other than the riot of emotion he invoked within her. 'The press, the Internet trolls.'

'You're such a liar, Hester. No, you're not. You never would have put yourself in their firing line if you really were. Tell me the real reason.'

'Words *can* hurt,' she argued.

'Maybe. Sometimes.' He nodded. 'Depending on who's doing the talking, right?'

He was very right. And now her voice was stolen by memories she had no wish to recall.

The teasing light in his eyes dimmed and he stepped closer. 'You can tell me,' he assured her quietly. 'I know you're prickly, you won't believe even the littlest of honest compliments. I know you don't let many people into your life.' He paused. 'I know this is an arrangement. I know I'm effectively paying for your company. And I know I tease you…but you *can* trust me. I hope that you might be able to trust me enough to be able to tell me *why* you've built such high barriers.'

She knew she shouldn't let the past constrain her future. And even though she had no real future with him, there was here and *now*. And she didn't want to lie to him any more. 'Because I've had my trust broken before.'

He waited, watching her. She knew she didn't have to explain it to him if she really didn't want to, but he was patient and quiet and somehow compelling.

'You're right,' she growled. 'I'm not really worried about the cameras or all the crowds or the online commentators. It's my three cousins.' She breathed out. 'I shouldn't have invited them.'

'You don't see them much?'

'I haven't seen them in years.' She didn't want to tell him how weak and vulnerable she'd been. And it wasn't all their fault, right? She probably hadn't made enough effort and they couldn't understand her and it had been too easy for her to shut down.

'I know no one is perfect, but they pretty much are.' She glanced at him quickly, offering superficial detail. 'And I wasn't. I was like a troll in the elven realm. They were a party of extroverted sporting elite. I liked reading in the corner. We just couldn't relate.'

He blinked, his expression perplexed. 'But how did they break your trust?'

She'd forgotten she'd admitted that first. She swallowed. 'With words.'

It wasn't a lie—it was very true. But it wasn't all of the truth.

'They've all accepted the invitation. They're here,' he said after a while. 'I've put them up at the hotel, rather than the palace. I've already issued a personal request that they don't speak to the media but I can't muzzle anyone completely. If they get seduced by the offer of an exclusive with a news agency—'

'I know.' She licked her lips nervously. 'I know you can't control everything.'

Of course they'd accepted the invitations. Who could turn down a flight in a private jet to attend something so high profile in the incredible country of Triscari? Even she hadn't been able to turn down his offer.

'I'm sorry I can't,' he murmured. 'I'm sorry they hurt you.'

She stiffened, holding back that yearning opening within with every step he took closer towards her. She didn't want his sympathy. She didn't want to think about any of that.

'But I'm not going to do that,' he added. 'I'm not saying anything I don't mean to you. When I talk about our inevitability, Hester, I'm not trying to flatter you. I'm just being honest.'

The trouble was his honesty was so naturally charming, so instinctively seductive. And while he was arrogant and confident, she didn't think even he really realised his potency. He was used to it, wasn't he? Flirting and having affairs. She just wasn't. She didn't think she could handle him.

'There are still only two kisses in our contract,' she breathed, clinging to that flimsy fact.

She had to keep him at that wafer-thin distance. He couldn't change the agreement before they'd even signed the marriage certificate.

'Trust me, I know.' He remained close for the merest moment more. 'And for what it's worth, I think you're going to slay them all tomorrow.'

Truthfully all she wanted was to slay *him*.

Fairy tales indeed.

CHAPTER SIX

HESTER SWAYED GENTLY as the glass carriage carried her along the castle route with its cobblestones and beautiful flower-strewn path to her waiting prince. The fine lace veil covering her face softened her focus so the vast crowds waving and watching blurred, but they were all there hoping to catch a glimpse of her—Prince Alek's mysterious bride.

She'd slept surprisingly well in the large wooden castle. Fiorella had arrived there too late in the evening for them to catch up and then Billie and her team had arrived first thing, along with an army of dressmakers. So she'd had no chance to talk to Fiorella—they were both too busy being beautified for the wedding. This was good because when she'd first spotted her soon-to-be sister-in-law, she'd veered dangerously close to hugging her. And Hester didn't hug anyone.

Before getting ready this morning she'd read only a few of the news stories about her that had been printed over the last few days. They'd not had that much time to dig up too much drama, but there was enough to make her shiver. But, worse, the real truth was there—some whispered of Alek's requirement to marry. That he'd picked someone biddable and shy and inoffensive. 'The bland bride', some bitchy bloggers had labelled her.

The romantics on the other side, however, wanted to believe the fairy tale and drowned out that truth with the fantasy. Their outing to the hospital had silenced many doubters and the body-language experts had had a field day. Apparently their light touch and laughing smiles showed 'intimacy and genuine love' between them.

And her moment with that distressed boy had somehow been leaked—still images taken by a long-range lens through a window while one of the teachers had spoken on condition of anonymity and talked of her natural affinity with the children...while Alek was apparently smitten and protective. Hester had put the tablet down, unwilling to read any more.

'We're almost there. Deep breath, Hester.' Fiorella smiled. 'This is going to be amazing.'

Contrarily Fiorella's soft reassurance sharpened Hester's nerves. Too late she realised the princess had been abnormally quiet all morning. Was she worried—or pre-occupied? 'Are you okay Fiorella?'

'Okay?' The princess's deep brown eyes widened and curiously a rush of colour swept into her cheeks. 'You mean about the wedding?'

What else would she have meant? Fiorella's gaze dipped but before Hester could ask more, the carriage slowed and then stopped.

'You're the best person in the world for Alek,' Fiorella whispered quickly before a footman appeared at the door.

Hester was glad of the veil—it gave her soft focus too. She could literally hide behind it.

She climbed the stone steps slowly as instructed, though mainly it was because the silk train of her dress was heavy. Then she saw Alek waiting at the end of the long aisle and was unable to tear her gaze from him. Every step drew her closer to him and revealed more detail of his appearance. He wore full royal regalia—gleaming gold trim, military medals and that scarlet sash of power across his chest and, yes, even one feather. He stood straight and strong and so serious, but as she finally drew alongside him she saw the smile in his eyes and a teasing twitch of his lips.

The ceremony was full of pomp just as he'd promised. There were trumpets, choirs, a cellist...but she barely noticed them. Nor did she really see the beautiful floral arrangements and the stunningly attired guests. *He* sucked all her attention.

It seemed to take for ever, yet passed in a flash. She was vitally aware of him breathing beside her, so close yet distant, and every moment watched by millions. She grew stupidly nervous after reciting her vows. Her mouth dried and she swallowed back her anxiety. Why had she shot down the idea of a practice kiss? They'd probably bump noses, or clash teeth or something even more awkward in front of the world. It was mortifying. And it would be replayed over and over, immortalised in memes on the Internet for ever. The 'world's worst kiss'.

Terrified, she looked at Alek. That knowing glint of good humour in his eyes grew and his lips curved enough to set the dimples free. She couldn't hold back her own impish smile in response. This whole thing? It *was* ridiculous. And suddenly it was fun, this secret contract between them.

He bent nearer, so very slowly. Utterly still, she expected only a brief peck.

It was a gossamer brush of his lips over hers, so gentle that she wouldn't have been sure it had happened if she hadn't seen him. But he lingered and her eyes drifted shut as intimacy was unleashed in that lightest, purest of touches. She yearned to capture it—to stop time and bask in the warmth and connection from such slight pressure.

He pulled back and smiled again right into her

eyes as she blinked and returned to the world.
The roaring cheers of the crowd seeped through
the stone walls and a ripple of audible pleasure
ran through the guests present in the magnificent palace chapel. He drew her hand through
his arm and escorted her down the long aisle.
The noise of the applause boomed tenfold as the
church door was opened for them to exit. They
stood for a long moment on the top step, smiling
at the scores and scores of people—the crowd
stretched as far as she could see.

'Hester.'

She heard his soft command and faced him.
The wicked laughter in his eyes was for her alone.

'Steel yourself, sweetheart,' he muttered.

She was ready and more willing than she
wanted to admit. But he knew, didn't he? She saw
the triumph in his eyes as he bent towards her.

This kiss lingered. This kiss lit something
else—there was more than a gossamer caress,
there was a hint of intent and she couldn't stop
her own response—the parting gasp of delight
that allowed him in.

But instead he pulled back. She saw his face
only briefly but the smile was gone from his
eyes—replaced by blazing intensity and an arrogant tilt to his jaw and suddenly he was back.
Stealing a third. This last kiss was not chaste.
He crushed her lips with his in a too-brief stamp

of passion that promised so much more than it ought to—the sweep of his tongue commanding a response that she couldn't withhold. Heat and power surged through her as his hands tightened—holding her firm while promising even more. Still dignified, but so, so dangerous. It was only a moment, but one that changed her irrevocably. Because she'd been the one to moan in regret when it ended. She'd never wanted it to end.

'That was three, not two,' she breathed, trying to whip up some fury but failing. She was too floored, too unstable in containing her feelings.

'So sue me,' he breathed back before laughing delightedly. 'What are you going to do about it standing here in front of the world?'

'Stop it, all the lip-readers will interpret what you're saying and they'll know this is—'

'You stop talking. I'm not even moving my lips. Ventriloquising is a talent of mine. Learned it from a very early age. You do when you're filmed and photographed at every possible opportunity.'

She giggled as she knew he'd intended. 'Is it even a word?'

'You bet. Formal study required.' He turned his head so no cameras could get between either of them and gazed into her eyes; his own were dancing. 'Now seriously, be silent, or I'll have to employ emergency tactics and I don't know that it would be wise for me to do that here and now.'

His voice had an edge and she knew what he meant. He raised his free hand and waved to the crowds, who cheered again, then he helped her down the marble steps and into the glass carriage. He sat close, his arm tight around her while she rationalised that extra kiss. He was pleased with the afternoon's events, that was all. That kiss had been a moment of pure male satisfaction—of pleasure and power.

'Hester?'

'No.' She glinted at him. 'You've had more than your lifetime allowance.' She smiled and waved to the crowd.

'But—'

'You can't ventriloquise your way out of this, Alek,' she scolded. 'You broke the deal.'

'Why, Hester Moss, are you chastising me?'

'I'm no longer Hester Moss.' She flashed her teeth at him in a brilliant smile. 'And I'm putting on a good show, aren't I?'

The woman formerly known as Hester Moss was putting on far more than 'a good show'. She was glittering. And almost flirting. And Alek discovered he could hardly cope. All he wanted was to pull her back into his arms and kiss her again. Again. And again. And ideally everywhere. Instead he had to smile and wave and grit his teeth because there were millions watching them.

In the safe privacy of a palace antechamber, he studied the tablet for the few minutes they'd factored ahead of the formal reception, taking time to settle his own rioting emotions the way he knew Hester did—with distraction and avoidance. But he couldn't deny her radiance—or his primal response to her.

He realised now—far too late—that he hadn't noticed any other woman in days and he *always* noticed women. Now he didn't seem to give a damn. He hadn't even seen them. And it wasn't just about ensuring Hester's comfort in a difficult situation. It was as if she were some giant magnet, while his eyeballs were iron filings. With no will of their own they just kept focusing on her. It was as if she'd obliterated anyone else out of existence. He laughed a little bitterly to himself. Served him right, didn't it? That he hadn't wanted a wife at all, but now he had one and he wanted his wife more than he'd wanted any other woman? And she was so off-limits—she was effectively an employee, she was a virgin, she was clearly vulnerable because she'd been hurt somehow and was isolated now…yes, the reasons why he shouldn't lay a finger on her were probably insurmountable. But that didn't stop his body from wanting her anyway.

'Are you okay?' she asked.

'Oh, I'm dandy,' he mocked himself. And he had to survive spending the night with her in his wing because there was no way they could sleep in separate apartments on their wedding night.

Was it only because she was out of bounds? As if he truly were some spoilt child who was so used to getting everything that he wanted that he couldn't cope the first time he'd heard the word no from a woman?

No. He simply ached to seduce her. He'd been skimming closer to seducing her with every passing day, more deeply intrigued as she'd opened up so fractionally, so slowly. Those sparks of humour, of spirit, fascinated him. He wanted to break her open and bask in the warmth and wit he knew she kept locked inside. And he wanted to test the intensity of this chemistry that made mush of his synapses, made every muscle tense and turned his guts to water.

Instead he had to endure a long celebratory feast in front of hundreds.

He glanced up from the screen and saw her hips and the curve of her bottom and was hit by a rush of lust so severe he had to freeze. No. It wasn't anything as superficial as simply being told he couldn't have something and only then wanting it. He wasn't a child any more. He'd outgrown the pursuit of challenges just for the sake of toppling them. This was all about her. He wanted to see her melt in pleasure. He wanted her to turn to him, to offer him her luscious mouth again. He wanted to coax more of the passion he'd discovered just beneath her still surface.

Instead he glared back at the screen.

The world was absolutely lapping it up—they were trending on all social media sites. Images of them spiralled throughout the web—one picture, just after the kiss, was being shared hundreds of thousands of times a second, it seemed.

When she'd smiled at him, it was like a revelation—all sparkle and beauty. It helped that her dress fitted as if she'd been poured into it— cinched at her waist and flaring over her full hips. It was absolute femininity. She was no rail-thin princess but rather a slim bundle of curves that were almost too sexy for the circumstance. The heels gave her a little extra height but she still barely made it to his shoulder. Her hair had been left mostly loose—all lush, lightly curled beauty—while the fragile tiara with its droplet diamonds added to the overall picture of princess perfection. How had he ever thought she wasn't beautiful?

'What is it?' She stepped over and he tilted the tablet so she could see them too.

She assessed the pictures silently, critically, showing no obvious emotion, but he knew she was thinking and feeling. He craved to know what. His heart still beat horrifically fast. Those two kisses had been the most chaste of his life— yet somehow the most erotic and they'd forced him into stealing that third. That too-brief statement of what he really wanted—to get her alone, away from all the watching people.

As alone as they were now.

He gripped the tablet tightly, resisting the wave of desire ricocheting through him. And the fierce regret. He wanted to start again. To forget the whole damn marriage requirement and instead take the simple pleasure of seducing her slowly and completely. All he wanted was her absolute surrender—for her to be his in the most basic sense of the word. She was the most exquisite temptation—a mystery, as the press had rightly labelled her. But the contract between them imposed rules and boundaries. He wanted to break every one here and now. It was appalling—he'd never imagined that she'd fascinate him so.

'It's amazing what properly fitting clothes and expertly applied make-up can do,' she muttered, oblivious to his turmoil as she swiftly scrolled through the photographs. 'I look okay.'

The dress and make-up merely accentuated the perfection beneath. 'I thought you didn't care what they think.' He managed to push through his tension to half-smile at her.

'Well, I don't want to let you down.'

'So you care what *I* think?' he asked more harshly than he intended.

She drew a slow breath and he knew she was settling her response to him, trying to keep her façade still. 'I care about doing a good job.'

'And that's all this still is to you? Just a job?' He didn't want to believe that. He refused to.

He fought the urge to haul her close—to make her flush, to make that serenity flare in a burst of satisfaction. He ached to see her shudder, to hear her scream as ecstasy overcame her. He wanted her warm and soft and smiling, no more cool, fragile façade. That first kiss had given him the briefest hint of what pleasure they could find together and had seared his nerve endings. He wanted to crack her open and release the warmth he was now certain was at her core.

They'd effectively laughed their way back down the aisle with an intimacy built on something other than physical. It had rendered him unable to resist the need to kiss her the way he'd ached to—stealing that third kiss to feel the heat of her response.

Now she was attempting to rebuild her personal barriers, to hide the fiercely deep feelings she didn't want to express. But she wasn't going to be able to deny them for too much longer. He'd felt the ferocity of her fire.

'I'm sorry about the article,' she said quietly, sidestepping his question.

'Your cousins.' He knew the one she meant. 'They said you ghosted them,' he said. 'That you emotionally shut them out.' He watched her expression stiffen and strove to reassure her. 'Hester, I of all people know not to believe everything I read in the media.'

'But it's true.' She lifted her chin but didn't meet his eyes. 'I did.'

Defensiveness radiated from every pore and his arms ached with the urge to hold her close.

'I'm sure you had good reason to,' he said carefully.

Now liquid gleamed in her eyes and smote his heart.

'It was silly, wasn't it? To have expected them to care for me, just because of blood.'

He took in what she'd said. They hadn't cared for her—they hadn't wanted her. And she'd been so unhappy she'd run away and locked herself in that ivory tower at the university. Quietly assisting students who lived fuller lives and cared less for their studies than she did.

'I didn't think they'd speak to the press.' Her whisper rushed. 'I thought inviting them would…' She shook her head. 'I should have known better.'

'They've gone the "friend of the family"

route,' he said, cynically aware of how the media worked. 'So they can say it wasn't them.'

'But it was.' She looked at him directly and he saw the hurt she'd tried to bury. 'I'm sorry if they've caused problems.' She pressed her lips together. 'Do I have to see them?'

'There's a receiving line.' He nodded. 'There'll be other eyes and ears but no cameras. We'll keep them moving quickly. I'll be on one side of you. Fi will be on the other.'

'She's been wonderful today.'

'She understands what it's like.' Alek nodded, but the strain was still etched on her face.

'She said she wants to stay in the States,' she murmured.

He let her lead the distraction, realising she needed it. 'Yes. I want her to do whatever she wants. She seemed distracted, said it's because she's thinking of doing postgraduate study.'

'She's super capable,' Hester agreed softly before turning her gaze back on him. 'What would you have chosen?' She inched closer. 'To do, I mean.'

'The crown chose me, Hester. That's why we're here.'

'But if you were free? If you didn't have to be a full-time royal?'

The wildness clawing inside him soothed a little under her gaze. He'd always wanted Fi to have the freedom he couldn't have. It was the sacrifice he'd made and he didn't regret it. What he regretted right now was the tension lingering around Hester's beautiful eyes. He never talked about all this impossibility; there was no point. But he desperately needed to stop thinking about kissing her. Distraction from difficulty was always good. And he needed to distract her too. Because that was what she was really asking him to do. So he did.

'I wanted to study medicine,' he blurted.

'You wanted to be a doctor?' Her jaw dropped and as she snapped it shut a frown furrowed her brow. 'How was that going to work?'

'I know, right? The idealism of youth.' He shook his head.

'It was a good ideal.' She curled her hand on his arm. 'You would have been—' She shook her head and broke off. 'What stopped you?'

'My father.' He smiled ruefully. 'I didn't ever think he'd disapprove of such a worthy profession, right? Literally trying to save people's lives.'

'You wanted to save lives?'

Dredging this up was infinitely preferable to facing the unrequited lust shivering through him like a damn fever. And thinking of this made him feel nothing but cold.

'I watched cancer slowly suffocate my mother, stealing her vitality and joy. It was horrendous

and there was nothin...
hated feeling so inept...
useless again.' He glos...
memories of his life. 'A...
ence. But my father did...
grades—before Mother g...
mucked around.'

He'd not discussed his .... death with anyone, ever. Yet it was somehow easier to talk about this than acknowledge the storm of emotion swirling within him. And Hester was in a realm of her own now in his life. Maybe he was a fool but he felt he could trust her. Besides, she'd lost both her parents and that was a pain he couldn't imagine.

'What happened to her motivated me. I wanted to make a difference and I finally got my head together. I was so proud when I got the grades that guaranteed my entry into medical school. I presented them to him. I thought he'd be proud too.'

'But he wasn't?' she whispered.

Her words somehow pushed aside the mocking self-pity to salve the true hurt beneath. He'd laughed it off to himself in recent years, but it had never really been a joke. It had broken his heart.

'He said it would take far too long to study. Eight years, minimum, before any real speciality. I had to devote more time to my country. You can't be King and have a career. Your career *is*

...ven though I didn't expect to take ...for a long time.' He shrugged. 'So ob- ...ly I couldn't do veterinary school either. ...rses were my other passion.' His stud farm on the neighbouring island was world renowned. 'I learned to ride before I could walk.' He made himself brag with a brash smile because he regretted bringing this up.

The lingering empathy in her eyes told him she still saw through to his old hidden pain but then she smiled. 'And what other amazing accomplishments does a prince have to master? Geography, I bet. Languages?'

'Five.' He nodded.

'Ventriloquism being one of them?' Her smile quirked.

'Of course.' That tension in his shoulders eased.

'Piano? Art?'

'Actually I do play the piano but I can't draw.'

'Well, I'm glad to discover you do have an imperfection or two,' she teased. 'So what did you do after he said no to everything you wanted?'

'I went into the military. Always acceptable. I trained with both navy and land-based forces.'

'But not air? You mean even with all your amazing accomplishments you can't fly a plane?'

'I occupied my very little spare time with polo. And other off-field pursuits.'

'Women.'

'I was going to say partying.' He maintained his smile through gritted teeth. 'I was bored and bitter and I felt stuck. I resented him for saying no to every damn thing that I truly wanted to do. So I did my work, but I had frequent blow-outs—and, yes, in part it was to piss him off.' He glanced at her ruefully. 'Predictable, right?'

'I can understand why you'd resent him and want to rebel. It's horrible being denied what you want all the time.'

'It is.' He glanced at her again and smiled faintly to himself. 'I'd wanted to do something meaningful and I wasn't allowed.' He sighed. 'I was angry. I was angry that Fi was so constrained. I was angry that he was always so distant and no matter what I did it was always a disappointment. He disapproved of my straight As, for heaven's sake. What was left to do other than rebel? But then it just became a habit and what everybody expected. It sure kept Triscari in the news—I maintained our high profile. There were just other consequences as well.'

'You were lonely,' she said softly.

'Hester.' He rolled his eyes. 'I was surrounded by people.'

'People who you couldn't really talk to. Your father was distant. Fi was too young and then you helped her get away to study, your mum had gone, there was nothing but party women and yes-men. I think that would get lonely.'

He rubbed his shoulder. 'You're too generous, Hester. I revelled in being the Playboy Prince.'

She studied him. 'You still want to do something meaningful?'

'My only job now is to be a good king for my country. I was angry about the marriage thing but perhaps, now it is done, I can get on and prove that this will all be good.'

'I don't think you need to prove yourself, Alek,' she said. 'I think what you do is very meaningful.'

He had no idea how the conversation had got so sidetracked. He'd meant to distract her from her distress about her family and himself from his desire for her. Yet somehow this had turned heavy and he'd told her far more than he'd intended. And somehow she'd soothed an old wound within him that he hadn't realised was still aching.

He gazed at her—her beautiful leonine eyes were more luminous than ever and how was it he wanted her more than ever? The ache to lean close, to touch her, was unbearable.

Instead he put down the tablet and stalked towards the door, remembering far too late that they had a palace full of people to please. 'We'd better get this over with.'

CHAPTER SEVEN

HESTER WATCHED HER husband charm everyone—hustling the receiving line through while making every guest believe he'd paid them extra special individual attention. She was fascinated by his skill—and so busy contemplating what he'd told her, the depth of his secrets and sadness and sacrifice, that she didn't spot her cousins until they were right there, confronting her with their fake smiles and stabbing eyes.

All the noise of the room receded as Joshua, Kimberly and Brittany stared at her. Hester froze, struck dumb as Kimberly executed a tart curtsey that exuded total lack of respect.

'Thanks for the invitation.' Brittany's faux polite opener was so barbed.

Hester still couldn't speak. They were older yet hadn't changed a bit. And how was it that they could make her feel so inept and small, even here and now?

'Our pleasure.' Alek filled the small silence

and extended his hand to Joshua. 'We're grateful you could join us in celebrating our special day.'

In the face of Alek's ruthless charm the three of them were rendered speechless. Hester watched with relief as they continued on into the reception room. It was good they'd shut up, but *she'd* not silenced them. And to her horror she discovered she still cared just a tiny bit too much. But Alek held her hand tightly, glued to her side in an outrageous display of possessiveness and protectiveness that she was enjoying far too much.

'I instructed Fi to spread the rumour that we're sneaking away early,' he muttered near her ear as they took to the dance floor. 'Which we are, by the way.'

'Okay.' It was silly to feel nervous. This wasn't a *real* wedding night, but a charade.

Less than thirty minutes later they walked through the corridors to their private apartments. 'You'll have to stay with me tonight,' he said softly. 'I'll sleep...'

'On the sofa?' she finished for him.

'Something like that.'

'We survived.'

'We did more than survive, we nailed it. Did you see their faces? They loved it.' He threw her a satisfied smile.

'Wonderful.' She'd hardly noticed anyone else. She'd hardly eaten anything at the dinner. And she'd managed only a couple of mouthfuls of champagne.

She glanced around his apartment, taking in the details to divert her thoughts. The set-up was similar to her own, only his had been refurbished in a modern style—no old-fashioned gaudy wallpaper for him.

'I might go straight to bed,' she murmured awkwardly.

'That's what you want?'

She froze. She couldn't even swallow.

His expression suddenly twisted. 'Relax, Hester. It's okay. Take the bedroom, second door on the left.'

She ought to have felt relief; instead hollow regret stole her last smile. But she'd only taken two steps into the bedroom when she realised the problem. Heat beat into her cheeks, but there was no getting around it. She walked back out to the lounge. Alek was exactly where she'd left him, staring moodily at the table.

'I'm going to need help to get out of this dress,' she said.

He lifted his chin and speared her with that intense gaze.

'I'm sewn into it.' She bit her lip, so embarrassed because it felt stupidly intimate and he seemed reluctant to move nearer. 'I'm sorry.'

'No, it's okay.' He cleared his throat and walked over to her. 'Let me see.'

She turned her back, so crazily aware that she held her breath as he ran his finger down the seam of her dress.

'I think I need scissors or something,' he said.

'You could always use your ceremonial sword.' She tried to lighten the atmosphere but it didn't work. Nothing could ease the tension she felt.

'Or my teeth,' he muttered.

She tried to quell her shiver but his hands stilled on her skin. For an endless profound moment, awareness arced between them.

'Come on,' he finally growled. 'I have scissors in the bathroom.'

He meant the bathroom that was en suite to his massive bedroom. Hester hovered on the edge of the room, trying not to stare at that huge bed, while he retrieved the scissors. Then she turned her back to him again.

'I don't want to ruin it,' he said in a low voice that purred over her.

She closed her eyes. 'I'm not going to wear it again—it won't matter if it gets a little torn.'

He worked silently for a moment longer. 'They'll put it on display at the palace museum eventually.'

'Really?' Even with her back to him his magnetism almost suffocated her. She wanted him to touch her more. She wanted another kiss…

'I really need to get out of this dress,' she begged desperately. 'I can't breathe any more.'

'Then let's get you out of it.'

She felt a tug and then he swore. 'I ripped a button off. Sorry.'

'It's fine.'

She heard his sharp intake of breath. And then she heard another unmistakable tearing sound. Her dress loosened, then slipped and she clutched the bodice to her chest. Gripping the silk tightly against her, she slowly turned to face him.

He was so near, so intent, so still. And she could so relate. She had to stay still too or else she was going to tumble into his arms like some desperate, over-sexed…*virgin*.

'Hester…'

She stared up at him.

'Just so we're clear,' he said softly. 'I didn't steal the third kiss for the cameras.'

She didn't move. She couldn't.

'It was pure selfish want on my part. I know I ought to apologise, but I think you enjoyed it as much as I did.'

He was so close she could feel his breath on her skin.

'I want to think you want another,' he said. 'Not on any stupid contract. Not limited.'

She couldn't reply.

'Your lips clung to mine.' Emotion darkened his eyes as he stared down at her, solemn and so intense, pressing his will on hers. 'I think you want me to kiss you and I sure as hell want to kiss you.'

He still didn't move. But he was right. She wanted him to touch her again. She ached to feel the electricity that had sizzled in that too-brief kiss. She wanted to know if it was real or if she'd imagined it. She *needed* to know that. 'Yes.'

'Yes?'

She knew he was warring within himself the same way she was.

'I do.' She whispered a vow more honest than the other one she'd given today.

He swooped down on her instantly. She'd never know how it happened but somehow she was backed up against the wall and he was kissing her and she was kissing him back as best she could because everything she'd been holding back for so long was released in a massive rush. All the want. All the heat. Sensual power burgeoned between them. She could no longer think, she no longer cared about anything other than keeping him kissing her. Keeping him close.

'Tell me to stop,' he groaned, lifting his head to gaze at her. 'Or do you want me to keep going? You know what I want, Hester. And while I'd like to think I know what you want, I *need* to hear it from you.' His breathing was rough but the touch of his hands at her waist was so gentle. 'I need to hear your voice.'

Even though she really wanted to, she couldn't make herself answer. She was so locked inside herself because what she wanted was so huge and she wanted it so much, she was terrified to ask for it.

'Hester?' His hands tightened on her waist.

As she gazed at the restraint in his eyes a trickle of power ran through her veins. And that trickle was enough to make her walls crack.

'I'm stronger than you,' he growled. 'I have you pinned against the wall. I could—'

'It's fine.'

His pupils flared. 'It's *what*?'

'Fantastic,' she corrected in a desperate rush. 'Please, Alek...'

She needed his touch—needed him to take her, *completely*. She wanted all of him for just this one night. Because she was so tired of being alone. She'd not realised how lonely she was until he walked into her life and made her want all kinds of impossible things. Things she could never have for good, but maybe just for now. Just for a night.

'Please what?' he growled, leaning closer. 'Tell me, Hester. I need you to tell me.'

He remained locked before her, waiting—silently *insisting*. His fierce expression forced her own fiery need to burst free.

'I'm *tired* of feeling nothing,' she cried at him breathlessly. 'I want to feel good. *This* feels good. I want to feel more good. Like *this*. With you.'

His eyes widened but he nodded. 'Okay.'

He lifted his hands from her waist to her wrists. She was holding her dress tightly to her chest but she knew what he was about to do. He applied gentle pressure to her wrists; he pulled her arms away from her body, making her beautiful dress slither to the floor. The tight bodice had meant she'd not needed underwear so now her breasts were bared. His coal eyes blazed into hers for a long moment before his gaze then lowered. His tension tripled as he stared at her. Stark, savage hunger built in his expression—an echo of her own. With a muffled groan he bent and pressed his mouth to her—kissing, caressing, caring. Unable to resist, she leaned back against the wall, shuddering with the intensity of the sensations he was arousing in her with every hot breath, each slide of his tongue and tease of his fingers. Her body arched as she was lost in the delight of it. Of *him*. He was so overpowering, so perfect.

'Oh…' She closed her eyes as his hands roved lower.

She was almost scared at how incredible it felt. 'Alek.' She couldn't stand it any more. *'Alek.'*

'Yes,' he muttered, as breathless as she. 'Yes, darling.'

She tumbled into incoherence, into nothing but heat and light, burgeoning sensations of pleasure and want. She arched against him as he slipped his hand beneath her silk panties, writhing until he had to hold her hips still with a hard hand so he could pleasure her, so he could coax her to the very crest of that most incredible feeling. He stroked her hard until she shook in his arms and screamed out the agony of ecstasy.

'You are *so* hot,' he said as he picked her up and carried her to his bed as if she weighed nothing. 'I knew you were.'

She didn't care what he knew, she just needed him closer. She needed more. 'Alek.'

She pulled him down to her. She'd never been this close to anyone and she didn't want it to end yet, not now she'd only just begun to discover him. Her hand slid up his chest, gingerly spreading her fingers to explore him.

'You can touch me.' He drew a shaking breath. 'Anywhere you want. Anyhow.'

She realised he *wanted* her to touch him. As much as she wanted him to touch her. This was give and take. Desire and hunger. She slid her hand further and watched him tense with pleasure at her touch. And then all reticence fled and she was driven to discover more. She helped him out of his suit, relishing the slow revelation of his gorgeous body. She caressed every inch of his muscled beauty, pausing when she ran her fingers over a jagged scar on his rump—not wanting to hurt him but wondering what had happened. He smiled, pulling her closer, and she forgot her question in the heat and tease of his kisses. He'd locked her in a dungeon of desire—hidden deep inside the heart of the palace, she was a prisoner to the overwhelming lust he aroused.

'Please,' she whispered. Her throat was so dry the word hardly sounded.

'Hester,' he groaned. 'I need you to tell me what you want me to do.'

'I thought you didn't like being told what to do?' She shuddered as he slid his leg between hers.

'I can make an exception for you.' He gazed into her eyes, his hips grinding delightfully against hers in a slow, tormenting motion. 'Do you want me to kiss you?'

'Yes.'

So he did—so thoroughly and lushly that she arched, unable to resist the urges of her body. He kissed, not just her mouth, but her neck and her chest. He kissed, nipped and nibbled, working his way lower and lower, kissing parts of her that had never been kissed before.

'Do you want me to touch you?' he breathed huskily against her belly.

'Yes.'

His hands swept over her—more and more intimately teasing and tormenting her until she writhed beneath him and even though he'd made her soar only minutes before, that empty ache inside was utterly unbearable.

And somehow he knew. He lifted himself up above her and looked directly, deeply into her eyes. 'Do you want me inside you?'

She wanted everything. Most of all she didn't want this good feeling to end. *'Yes.'*

But he didn't smile. 'You're sure?'

'This is like a dream, Alek. Just for tonight.'

'A dream?' He shook his head. 'This isn't a dream you can wake up from and take back, Hester.'

Her anger built. She'd not had this—not opened herself up to anyone—ever. And all she wanted was him. Now. And she didn't want him to make her wait any longer. 'Don't say anything more,' she moaned. 'Don't spoil it.'

He tensed.

'And don't stop,' she demanded fiercely. 'Yes. I want you.'

His smile spread across his face and then he kissed her again. Until she arched, until she moaned, until she couldn't form words. For a moment he paused—vaguely she realised he was protecting them both—but then he was back, big and heavy against her, and she revelled in it. He slid his hand beneath her bottom and held her still enough for him to press close. She gasped as she felt his thickness sear into her.

'Hester?' he breathed.

'Yes. Alek.' She wanted this. Him.

As he pushed closer still she trembled. He was so big and so strong and she was suddenly overwhelmed. But he moved so slowly, so carefully and then he kissed her again—in that deep, lush way, as if he'd wanted nothing more in all his life than to kiss her. As if she were the very oxygen he needed to survive. That was when everything melted within her and he slid to the hilt, so they were as deeply connected as they could possibly be. Her need coalesced again into a cascading reaction of movement. He pushed her to follow his sweet, hard, slick rhythm—into a dance she'd never known, but discovered she could do so damn well with him. His breathing roughened as she clutched him back, as she understood more the give and take, the meet and retreat of this magic. Together they moved faster, deeper…until she cried out as he brought unbearable, beautiful pleasure down upon her. As he broke through every last one of her boundaries to meet her right there—where there was light and heat and sheer physical joy.

And finally, when she couldn't actually move, when her body was so wrung out, so limp from that tornado of ecstasy, a small smile curved his gorgeous lips. He rolled but pulled her close, draping her soft body over his. And he kissed her again—a sweet intimacy she was still so unused to, and still so desperately hungry for. So hungry, in fact, that it took only one long, lush kiss to stir her hips into that primal circling dance again.

'Oh, Hester,' he muttered and swept his hands down her yearning body. 'You're magnificent.'

CHAPTER EIGHT

ALEK RESTED ON his side, watching her sleep—half impatient, half fascinated—until she finally stirred. Her gaze skittered away from his as she sat up. For the first time in his life he was unsure how to handle the morning after.

'Sorry I slept in.' She slithered from the bed and swiftly reached for the robe lying across the nearby chair. 'I had an amazing time. Thank you.'

Amazing? She had no idea what amazing was. But he supposed it was better than her telling him it had been 'fine'.

'No regrets?' He pushed for more than this awkward politeness from her.

'I don't think it would be right to regret something that felt that good.' She belted his favourite robe tightly around her waist, hiding her perfection from him again. 'I'll go back to my room now.'

'You don't have to,' he said huskily, rubbing a sore spot he felt in his chest.

Ordinarily he'd be relieved to have a lover leave him with such little fuss, but he wanted

Hester to stay. But every ounce of her shy reserve had returned.

'I know…but I…um…' She drew breath. 'My clothes are in there.' She silently sped from the room—as if she daren't leave a mark or a sound.

And he just let her.

He stared into the blank space. Breaking through her shell had been difficult and this morning it had just bounced back into place. Maybe she needed some time alone to process what had happened? Honestly, maybe he did too. Maybe letting her leave now might mean she'd be comfortable coming back soon.

Just this once.

That was what she'd whispered last night and if he were being sensible, that was how he'd leave this. But he rubbed his chest again as the reality of the situation hit hard. His sexual attraction to her hadn't been assuaged but exacerbated. Worse was his burgeoning curiosity about everything else about her. He wanted to understand it all— her bag and her box and the books she'd not kept. Why did she have so few belongings?

And the emptiness of his bedroom hurt. Suddenly he hated that she'd walked out on him. That he'd made it so easy for her to be able to. He should have stopped her. He should have seduced her. He should have stripped back her protective prickles again and found that hot, sweet pleasure with her.

He gazed out of the window, noting the blazing sun and blue sky. Personal temptation stirred harder. He'd just married for his country—didn't he deserve a few moments of private time?

He phoned his assistant, Marc. 'I know we have meetings this morning, but I plan to take Hester to the stud this afternoon. Make the arrangements.'

'Sir?'

'Two nights,' he repeated. 'Make the arrangements.'

A minute later he knocked on the door of her apartment and turned the handle. 'Hester?'

She'd not locked it and he found her in the centre of her lounge, that wooden box in her hand. He watched as she awkwardly secured the loose lid in place with two thick rubber bands.

'Sorry,' she apologised and put the box on a nearby table. 'How can I help?'

He disliked her deferential attitude and the reminder of that 'contract' between them. Hadn't they moved past that last night?

'Come breakfast with me by the pool,' he invited. 'Then I have a few meetings, but this afternoon we're taking a trip. You'll need to pack enough for a couple of days.'

'A trip?' Hester could hardly bring herself to look at him; all she could think of was what they'd done last night. All night. How good he'd made her feel. 'I thought we had to stay in the city to oversee the coronation plans and practise everything a million times.' She doggedly tried to focus on their responsibilities. 'Do I really have to kneel before you all by myself?'

'All citizens of Triscari do, but especially the King's wife.'

'It's a wonder you don't want me to lie prostrate on the floor,' she grumbled.

'Well, of course I do, but perhaps not in front of everyone else.' He sent her a wicked double-dimpled look. 'We can do that alone later. Anyway, apparently the plans are in hand so we can steal a couple of days for a honeymoon.'

A honeymoon? Her stomach somersaulted. Was he joking? She stood frozen but he bent and brushed his lips over hers briefly, pulling away with a shake of his head.

'No.' He laughed. 'You can't tempt me yet.'

'I didn't tempt you,' she muttered. 'I didn't do anything.'

'Hester,' he chided softly. 'You don't have to *do* anything to tempt me.' He cocked his head and gave her a little push. 'Now, head to the pool. I'll meet you there shortly.'

Hester stretched out on a sun lounger, trying to read, but her brain was only interested in replaying every second of the previous night. Her body hummed, delighting in the recollections. She'd not realised the extent of what she'd been missing out on. No wonder people risked so much for sex. But she knew it would never be like that with just anyone. It hadn't just been Alek's experience or 'expertise'. It had felt as if he'd cared—not that he was in love with her, of course, but that he was concerned for her feelings, for her to receive pleasure. That he desired to see her *satisfied*. She'd not had that courtesy, that caring, from anyone in so long. It was partly her own fault— she'd not let anyone get close in years. She'd not intended to let Alek get close either, but somehow he'd swept aside all her defences. Swiftly. Completely. So easily.

She knew sleeping with her meant nothing truly meaningful to him, not really. This was merely a bonus to their arrangement. She'd consider it that way as well. She could keep her heart safe—not fancy that she was falling for him, like a needy waif who'd never been loved…

But some distance right now was so necessary—which was why this talk of a honeymoon terrified her.

It's just one year.

And last night had been just that once. They'd blurred the lines and perhaps that had been inevitable. While she didn't regret it, she couldn't get carried away on a tide of lust and mistake his actions for meaning anything more than mere physical attraction.

But Alek fascinated *her* far beyond that. She'd instinctively believed he had more depth than he let show and she'd been right. He'd been hurt by his mother's death, frustrated by his father's control over him, protective of his sister. And now of her.

There was meaningful intention in most of his actions. The playboy persona was part rebellion, only one element of his whole. He was also honourable, loyal, diligent and he did what was necessary for his country.

Okay, yes, just like that she was halfway to falling for him.

She swam, trying to clear her head and ease the stiffness in her body. Lunch was delivered on a tray to the table beside her lounger. After eating, she went back to her apartment to pack. But when she went to put her wooden box in her bag, it wasn't on the table where she'd left it. She stared at the empty space, confused. She'd opened it only this morning, but now? She whirled, quickly scanning every possible surface but the box wasn't on any. She broadened her search but it was fruitless. Finally she hit panic point—repeating the search with vicious desperation, tipping out her bag and tearing up the place.

'Hester? What's happened?'

She froze. She'd not heard him knock and now he was in the middle of her mess with his eyes wide.

'It's missing.' She hugged herself tightly, but couldn't claw back any calm. 'I can't go.'

He didn't answer as he slowly stared around her room. Hester followed the direction of his gaze and realised what a mess she'd made of the place. She'd opened and emptied every cupboard and drawer in the apartment and still not found it. Cushions and pillows were strewn across the floor alongside books and blankets.

His focus shot back to her. 'Your box?'

'Yes,' she breathed, stunned that he realised what she meant so quickly. 'Who would take it?' Her anxiety skyrocketed all over again.

'You were going to pack it? You take it everywhere with you?'

'Yes.' She couldn't bear to lose it—it held everything.

A strange expression flashed across his face. 'Wait here. Just wait. Two minutes.'

'Alek?' Confused, she leaned against the wall, her arms still wrapped around her waist as his footsteps receded.

It was more than two minutes before he returned but she was locked in position, blinking back tears. She stared as she realised what he was holding. *'Why?'* Her voice cracked. 'Why would you take it?'

'I thought I could get it back before you noticed it was gone. I'm sorry for upsetting you.'

'Why would you—?' Furious, she broke off and struggled to breathe as she took the box from him and saw it close up. The lid was open while the interior was empty. Heat fired along her veins and her distress grew. 'Where's everything gone?'

'I have it all, just in my room. I'll get them now.'

'Why?' The word barely sounded but he'd already gone.

Hester sank onto the sofa, snatching a breath to study the box properly. She closed then reopened the lid. It didn't fall off any more, while the rubber bands were gone altogether.

Her bones jellified as she realised what he'd done.

Alek returned and carefully set a small tray on the low table in front of her sofa. It held everything she'd kept. All the little things. All her precious memories.

'The lid opens and closes again.' She blinked rapidly as he sat beside her. 'It has a new hinge.'

'Yes.' He cleared his throat. 'I took it this morning after you went to the pool. I thought…' He paused and she felt him shift on the sofa. 'I knew it was precious to you. I knew it was broken. So I—'

'Had it fixed.' Her voice almost failed.

'I wanted it to be a surprise…' He trailed off and blew out a breath. 'I should've asked you,' he muttered roughly. 'I'm so sorry. You probably loved it as it was.'

'Broken?' She shook her head and her words caught on another sob as she was unable to restrain the truth. 'It broke my heart when it happened.'

He gazed at her and the empathy in his eyes was so unbearable, she had to turn away from it.

'I can't even see where the crack was.' She stared hard at the box, refusing to let her banked tears tumble.

'We have an amazing craftsman—he maintains the woodwork in the castle. He's exceptionally skilled,' Alek explained.

'And so fast…' She ran her finger over the lid of the box. How had he done this in only a few hours?

'I talked to him about it before the wedding so he knew the issues.'

'Before the wedding?' Her heart skipped. He'd noticed her box and planned this?

'I wanted to get a wedding gift that you would like.'

Her throat was so tight it wouldn't work. That he'd thought to do this for her? It was more precious than any jewels, any other expensive, exquisite item. And she wasn't used to someone wanting to do something so nice for her.

'I didn't get you anything.' She finally looked at him directly, instantly trapped in his intent gaze.

He shook his head gently. 'You've done enough by marrying me, Hester.'

That was enough? Just that contract? Somehow she didn't want that to be enough for him. She wanted him to want more from her. That dangerous yearning deepened inside—renewed desire for that intimacy they'd shared last night. But he'd let her leave this morning. He'd barely said anything. Horribly insecure, she tore her gaze from his and turned back to the table, taking in the contents of the second tray.

'Did your craftsman put these here for you?' Her heart skidded at the thought. She needed to touch each talisman and make them hers again.

'No. I didn't want him going through your things,' he said softly. 'I took them out before giving him the box.'

Something loosened inside. She was glad it was only he who'd touched them. He'd been thoughtful and kind and suddenly the walls within crumbled and her truth, all her emotion, leaked out—sadness and secrets and sacrifice.

'The box was my father's,' she said quietly. 'Actually it was his great-grandfather's, so it's really old. It was for keeping a pocket watch and cufflinks and things. I loved it as a child and Dad gave it to me for my treasures. Marbles I had, sea glass I found. We found this piece together when I was…' She trailed off as she held the piece in her hand. Memories washed over her as they always did when she opened the box—which wasn't often at all purely because of the intensity of emotion it wrought within her. But it was also why she loved it, why it was so very precious and so personal and she couldn't help whispering the secrets of more. 'The pencil was my mother's.' It was only a stub of a pencil. And the remnant of the thin leather strap from her purse. 'You must think I'm pathetic.' She quickly began putting the other items away. 'All these broken little things—'

'What? No.' He put his hand on hers and stopped her from rapidly tossing everything back into the box haphazardly. Slowly he put one item at a time into her palm so she could return them to their special place.

'Everything around me,' Alek said quietly. 'This palace—my whole life—is a memorial to my family. There are portraits everywhere…everything is a reminder of who I am, where I'm from and who I must be. You don't have that, so you keep all these. There are treasured memories in every one, right?'

She nodded, unable to speak again. Emotion kept overwhelming her and she hated it.

He picked up the white-silk-covered button from the tray and held it out for her to take. 'I'm glad this was something you wanted to remember.'

He'd recognised it? She'd scooped it from the floor on her way out of his apartment this morning. Her fingers trembled as she took the button from her wedding dress and put it into the box.

'I'm never going to forget last night,' she whispered. Just as she was never going to forget anything associated with all her broken treasures. She closed the lid, amazed again at how perfect the repair was.

He watched her close the box. 'How did it get broken?'

She traced the carved lid with the tip of her finger as he'd done that day they'd met. 'It even used to lock. I wore the key around my neck on a ribbon, hoping they couldn't see it under my shirt.'

'They?'

'My cousins.' She shrugged. 'They didn't like it when I went to live with them after my parents died.'

'They didn't welcome you?' He paused.

'My aunt and uncle were sure to publicise that they'd "done the right thing" in taking me in. But they already had three children and none of them wanted me there.'

'So they didn't give you a nice room, or let you make their home your own.'

'No.' She swallowed. 'My uncle sold most of my parents' things, but I had the box. I always kept it near me. I never left it in my room or anything because I knew not to trust them. But the ribbon was worn and one day I lost it. They teased me about never being able to open the box again because I'd lost the key—so then I knew they had it and they knew I knew. That was their fun, right? My helplessness. My desperation. There was nothing I could do and they enjoyed that power.' She shivered. She'd hated them so much. 'So I tried not to show them how much it mattered.'

'I'm guessing you told them that it was "fine" for them to have it?' He rubbed her hand. 'That's your fall-back, right? When you don't want to say what's really going on inside there.' He pressed his fist to his heart.

She nodded sadly. 'My cousin Joshua snatched the box off me, he said he'd open it for me, but he was mocking and mean. He tried to prise it open by force but couldn't, so he got a knife. He broke the hinge and the lid splintered and everything fell on the ground. The three of them laughed at all my things. They said it was all just unwanted rubbish. All broken, with no value. Like me.'

Alek muttered something beneath his breath.

'I ran away,' she confessed sadly. 'There was nothing else I could do, I just ran.'

'I don't blame you.' He gazed at her, his dark eyes full of compassion that she couldn't bear to see, yet couldn't turn away from. 'I would've done the same.'

She shook her head with a puff of denial. Because he wouldn't have. He'd have fought them or something. He was so much stronger, so much more powerful than her. He'd never have let himself get stomped on the way she had. 'I went back hours later, when it was dark and it was all still there on the ground where they'd dumped it.'

'Hester—'

'I knew then that I had to get away for real.' Pain welled in her chest and she gazed down at the box. She'd never understood why they'd been so mean—what it was she'd ever done. Why it was that she'd not been welcomed.

'Were these the cousins who attended the wedding yesterday?'

She nodded.

'If I'd known…' He muttered something harsh beneath his breath. '*Why* did you invite them?'

'It would have caused more harm if I hadn't. Imagine what they'd have said to the media then?'

'I don't give a damn *what* they'd have said.'

'It's fine, Alek. They can't hurt me any more.'

He glanced at her. 'It's not *fine*, Hester. And you know that's not true.'

'Well...' she smiled ruefully '...they can't hurt me as much as they used to. I'm not a child. I'm not as vulnerable. I do okay now.'

'You do more than okay.' He blew out his tension. 'Were these the people who tested whether your eyelashes are real by pulling them out?'

She stared at him, her heart shrivelling at the realisation that he'd seen so much. 'How did you—?'

'No one normal would ever think to do that. You only mentioned it because some cruel witch had actually done it.'

She stared into space, lost in another horrible memory. 'It was girls at school,' she mumbled. 'Pinned me down.'

'At school?'

His horror made her wince.

'I got myself a scholarship to an elite boarding school. It was supposed to be my great escape— a wonderful fresh start away from the cousins.'

'And it wasn't?' He clenched his jaw.

'It was worse.'

She felt the waves of rage radiating from him and opted to minimise what she'd confessed.

'They were just mean. I ran away from the school. I worked. I studied. I did it myself.'

'You shouldn't have had to.'

'It's okay.'

'It's not okay, Hester.'

'But *I'm* okay. Now. I truly am.' And she realised with a little jolt that it was true. If she could handle getting married in front of millions of people, she could handle anything, right?

He looked into her eyes for a long moment and finally sighed. 'My craftsman said he'd fixed the lock too,' he said, drawing a tiny ornate key from his pocket. 'So now you can lock it again and keep it safe.' He held the key out to her. 'And you could put the key on a chain this time.'

She curled her fingers around the key and pressed it to her chest. 'This was so kind of you, Alek.'

His smile was lopsided so the dimples didn't appear and he didn't kiss her as she'd thought he was about to. Instead he stood.

'We need to get going or it'll be too dark.'

'Of course,' she breathed, trying to recapture control of herself, but there was a loose thread that he seemed to have tugged and still had a hold of so she couldn't retie it. 'I need a minute to tidy up.'

'The staff will tidy up.'

'I'm not leaving this mess for them.' She sent

him a scandalised look. 'They'll think we had a massive fight or something.'

He grinned as he scooped up an armful of pillows and put them away with surprising speed. 'Or something.'

CHAPTER NINE

HESTER GAZED UP at the double-storeyed mansion set in the centre of green lawns and established trees. 'I didn't think there could be anything more beautiful than the palace or the castle, but this is—'

'Very different from either of those places.' Alek said.

'Yes, it's…' She trailed off, unsure she wanted to elaborate; he seemed oddly distant.

Only then he wasn't.

'What?' He stepped in front of her, his gaze compelling. 'Tell me what you think.'

It was impossible to deny him anything when he stood that close.

'It doesn't seem like a royal residence. It's more like a home.' Admittedly a beautiful, luxurious home—but there was something warm and welcoming and *cosy* about it.

'It was home.' Something softened in his eyes. 'My mother designed it and my father had it built for her before I was born.' His lips twisted in a half-smile.

'You grew up here?'

He nodded. 'She wanted us here as much as possible. School had to be in the city, of course, but before then and every holiday during. It was our safe place to be free.'

Hester was fascinated and honoured that he'd brought her somewhere clearly so special to him. 'Was?'

'My father never returned here after she died.' He gazed across the fields before turning to walk towards the homestead. 'Because she died here.'

Hester stilled. But he strode ahead and clearly had no desire to continue the conversation.

She couldn't catch her breath as she followed him through the living area. The interior of the homestead was much more personal than the palace. Large, deep sofas created a completely different space—it was luxurious and comfortable and she felt as if she was encroaching on something intimate and deeply personal.

'You really love horses,' she muttered inanely when it had been silent too long and because out of every window she saw the beautiful animals grazing in the fields.

He chuckled at her expression. 'You've never ridden?'

NATALIE ANDERSON   185

'I'm nowhere near co-ordinated enough. I've seen video of Fiorella, though. She's amazing.'

'She likes show jumping. I prefer polo.'

'Whacking things with your big stick?' She smirked.

He eyed her, that humour and wickedness warming his gaze. 'At least I'm not *afraid* of them.'

'They're huge and powerful and they could trample me to death. Of course I'm afraid of them.'

'They'll sense your fear. Some will behave badly.'

'A bit like people, really,' she muttered.

'True.' He laughed as he led her up the stairs. 'Come up and appreciate the view. All the staff have gone away for these couple of nights so we're completely alone.'

His phone pinged and he frowned but paused to check the message.

'It never ends for you, does it?' she asked.

'I imagine it's the same for you,' he replied as he tapped out a quick reply. 'Students pulling all-nighters wanting help with their due essays. Fi's correspondence is mountainous.'

'I like being busy,' she said. 'I always took extra sessions at the drop-in centre.'

'What drop-in centre?' He glanced up and pocketed his phone. 'For the students?'

'No, an advice bureau in the city. I helped peo-ple fill in forms and stuff.'

'Is that where you sent that first tranche of money?'

'Yes.' She blushed. 'Something charitable, as you said. I couldn't ignore that.'

But his gaze narrowed. 'I had the feeling it was more than charitable. That it might've been personal.'

'Okay.' Her heart thudded; of course he'd seen that. 'You're right. I've asked the centre to give it to a young mother and her daughter,' she con-fessed. 'Lucia's on her own. She's trying to make a better life for her daughter. I used to hold the strap of my mum's bag the way Zoe holds Lu-cia's.'

Alek soaked up the information. The trust blooming in Hester's eyes was so fragile but he couldn't resist seeking more. 'Tell me about her—your mother.' He wanted to understand every-thing.

She looked at him, her golden eyes glowing with soft curiosity of her own. 'Tell me about yours,' she countered.

His jaw tightened, but at the same time his lips twisted into a reluctant smile. Her question was fair enough. 'Her name was Aurora and she was from a noble family on the continent. Apparently my father saw her riding in an equestrian event and fell for her instantly. She loved her horses so he built these stables for her to establish a breeding programme. It was his wedding gift to her.'

'Wow.'

'Yeah.' He nodded. 'They struggled to have me and it was a long time before they got Fiorella after me. So I'll admit I was very spoiled.'

'Everyone should be spoiled sometimes.' Hester suddenly smiled. 'Especially by parents, right?'

Warmth blossomed in his chest and he took her by the hand and led her to the second-storey veranda.

'My mother passed her love for horses on to me—they were our thing,' he said as he tugged her to sit down on the large sofa with the best view in the world—over horse-studded fields, to his favourite forest and the blue sea beyond. 'She had such a gift with them. Meanwhile, my father was very busy and dignified.' He rolled his eyes but was actually warming to the topic because he'd not spoken of her in so very long. 'She was vivacious—he was the shadow, the foil to her light.'

'They sound like they were good together.'

He stretched his feet out on the sofa and tucked her closer to his side, kind of glad he couldn't see her face, and he watched as the sky began to darken.

'Yeah, they were. She softened him, kept him human. But then she got sick. It was so quick. My father wouldn't reduce his engagements. Wouldn't admit what was happening. Wouldn't speak to me about it. But I was fourteen and I wasn't stupid. I stayed with her here. I'd bring the horses by her window downstairs and we'd talk through the programme...' He'd missed months of school that year.

'And Fiorella?'

'Came and went. She was young and my mother wanted to protect her. So did I. She'd go for long rides every day—she had a governess. And I sat with Mother and read to her. But she deteriorated faster than any of us expected. I wanted to call her specialists, for my father, but she wouldn't let me. It was just the two of us.'

The horror of that morning—that rage against his powerlessness resurged—breaking out of the tiny box he'd locked it in all these years. 'I couldn't help her. I couldn't stop it.'

What did titles or brains or money or anything much matter when you were reduced to being so completely *useless* in a moment of life and death? 'I couldn't do anything.'

He was still furious about it.

'You did do something, Alek,' Hester eventually said softly. 'You were *there* for her. She wasn't alone. Isn't that the best thing anyone could have done? You were *with* her.'

He couldn't answer.

'Nothing and no one can stop death,' she added quietly. 'And being alone in that moment must be terrifying. But she wasn't alone, because she had you. That's not nothing, Alek. That's about the furthest from nothing that you can get.'

He turned. In the rising moonlight her eyes were luminous. This was someone who knew isolation. Who understood it—within herself, and within him. And she was right. A slip of peace floated over his soul, slowly fluttering into place, like the lightest balm on an old sore, a gossamer-thin layer of solace.

He'd never allowed himself to think of that moment. Even the threat of recollection hurt too much. But now that memory screened slowly, silently in his head and for once he just let it.

'And then what happened?' Hester finally asked.

He looked at her blankly.

'Afterwards. Your father, Fiorella, you. How did you all cope?'

They hadn't. None of them had.

'Your father didn't come for you?' Hester asked.

'He never returned here.' Alek coughed the frog from his throat. 'He stayed at the palace and they brought her body to him. He made them bring me too.' He'd never wanted to leave. He'd wanted to hide here for ever. 'I fought to come back from then on because I didn't want the stables to close. People had jobs and there were the thoroughbreds...'

'And it was your mother's project,' she said.

'Right.' He released a heavy sigh. 'She loved it.' How could he let it fall to ruin? 'I didn't want to lose her legacy.'

But it had been hard to come back and see that small room downstairs where she'd spent her last days. Awful to be here alone when she'd gone for ever and his family had almost disintegrated.

'And Fiorella?'

'The governesses kept her away and kept her busy. She was okay. But as my father retreated into his work he became even more strict and controlling over our lives. Over every aspect. I guess it was his way of handling it.'

'And what was your way of handling it?' she murmured.

He flexed his shoulders. 'I didn't have one really.'

'No?'

'You're thinking my social life?' he asked—feeling weary and oddly hurt at the suggestion. 'Maybe. It didn't mean anything.'

'Maybe that was the point,' she said lightly.

'If it didn't mean anything, then it couldn't hurt, right?'

'Not gonna lie—it felt *good*, Hester.'

'Well, wouldn't it suck if it didn't?' She smiled. 'And when things really hurt you'll do almost anything to feel better even for a little while, right?'

He felt raw. Maybe she was right. Maybe it had been more than escape. He'd been burying frustration and grief. But he'd *liked* being the Playboy Prince. He'd liked encouraging zero expectations of him settling down. Only then his father had died. And then that stupid requirement had come into play and he'd been forced to create a relationship he'd never wanted. That he still didn't want—right?

'You don't need to apologise for it,' she said. 'It just was what was, right? I locked myself away. That was my choice. Neither of us were right or wrong necessarily, it was just how we each coped with a really crappy time.'

'Yeah.' He'd not stopped to think about what a really crappy time it had been in so long.

'So now you run the stud.' She looked across the grounds. 'And that was the other way of handling it—building on her legacy. Keeping something that she loved very much alive.'

He swallowed, unable to reply.

'And you freed Fiorella from that royal burden.'

'Of course I did.' He could breathe again. 'That was easy. She didn't need to be stuck in Triscari the same as...'

'The same as you.'

'It's just fate.' He shrugged. 'An accident of birth. I just have to do the best I can.'

'Do you worry about your ability to do the job?' She stared at him. 'Seriously?'

'What, you have dibs on feeling insecure?' He half chuckled. 'Of course I worry I won't be good enough. Being the firstborn Prince means you're going to end up King. It's a full-time job that starts from the moment you're born and it takes up every minute. I'm not saying that to summon your sympathy. I know how privileged I am and I want to do what's right for my country.'

'And you do. They love you. They ask for your thoughts all the time and they trust your answers. Everyone loves you. Everyone knows you do what's best for the country because you care. And as long as you keep caring, then you'll do what's right for Triscari. You're not selfish, Alek.' She paused. 'You've given your life for duty.'

He shot her a look. 'I thought I was a rapscallion playboy.'

'Maybe you were when you could snatch a second to yourself, but mostly you've done the job forced upon you. And the job you wanted to do for your mother.' Hester realised he couldn't separate his role as Prince from his *self*. It was a career like no other—too enmeshed with his very existence and it brought with it a kind of pressure she'd not stopped to consider. 'You're building on your father's legacy too, by being a good king. But you're more important than just your crown, you know—'

'I know,' he interrupted and reached out to stroke her hair back from her face. 'Don't worry too much, my ego is perfectly healthy.'

She actually wasn't so sure about that. 'But it's isolating, isn't it?' she said passionately. 'Living with grief.'

His eyes widened. 'I'm not—'

'Yes, you are. For your mother. For the life you're never going to be able to have.'

And somehow in the course of this conversation her own loneliness had been unlocked. 'I grieve for the life I might've had if the accident hadn't happened,' she confided in an unstoppable swirl of honesty. 'I was at the library, happily reading and waiting for them to pick me up. They never did and I never got to go home again. I was taken to the police station and after a few hours my uncle arrived and took me. Five hours of flight time later I landed in a place I didn't know, to meet people who didn't want me.'

Alek just stared at her, and this time his eyes were so full of care and compassion and she wanted to share with him—because it wasn't all awful. She'd been so lucky in so many ways.

'My parents were a runaway love match.' She smiled impishly, delighting in the romance they'd had. 'He was the second youngest, destined to uphold their place in society, right? His family were snobs. My mother was new to town, moved into the wrong suburb...she totally wasn't from the right background. They met at school and it was true, young love. But when she got pregnant his family came down so hard and they ran away— living transiently, working seasonal jobs, barely keeping themselves housed and fed, fighting hard to stay afloat and keep me with them. But they did it. They loved each other and they loved me. They decided they couldn't afford more so there was just me and...not going to lie, Alek...' she smiled cheekily at him '... I was spoiled too.'

'Oh, sweetheart,' he said huskily. 'I'm so glad to hear that.'

'Yeah, we had nothing but we had everything, you know? And we certainly never visited his home town. So after the accident when I turned up, all that old bitterness was still real. I didn't fit in—I looked more like my mother than my father. I had her vixen eyes. I was part of who and what stole him away and that made me bad. But they were determined to "do the right thing". Except they had nothing good to say about my mum and they went on about my father's selfishness and weakness. I couldn't tell them how wonderful they really were—they didn't want to listen and they never would've believed me. In the end the only way to get through it was to lock my grief away, shut it down.' She shook her head. 'I put everything into my studies, hoping that would lead to a way out, and eventually it did, but only once I got to university and by then... I was good at keeping others at a distance. I put the treasures into my box and I'd go for long walks.'

'Walks? *That* was your way to feel good?' He half laughed.

'Sure. Mostly...' She smiled more ruefully this time. 'But a couple of times I ran.'

'You shouldn't think running away is something to be ashamed of. Or that it's cowardly.'

'Isn't it though? Shouldn't I have stood up for myself or fought harder to be heard?'

'How were you supposed to do that when there were a tonne of them and only one of you?' He shook his head. 'I think what you did was actually more brave. Escaping that abuse, and going out on your own. Lots of people wouldn't have the courage or the skills to be able to do that without support.'

Alek hadn't known it was possible to feel supremely content and disconcerted at the same time. He was both assuaged and unsatisfied. Most of all he was confused. This was not the way he'd envisaged this evening going. He'd thought they'd have been in bed hours ago—that he'd have stripped her and satisfied them both several times already. Instead they'd shared something far more intimate than if they'd spent hours having simultaneous orgasms.

And somehow he couldn't stop speaking. 'Tell me more,' he asked. 'What were their names?'

To his immense relief she answered—and asked questions of her own. He shared old anecdotes he hadn't realised he'd even remembered. Making her laugh over silly, small things that were too personal to keep back. As the stars emerged he leaned back lower on the sofa, curling her closer into his side—soft and gentle and warm and appallingly tired and still talking.

Yet the discomfort was still there. All kinds of aches weighed down his limbs as he discovered that an old hurt he'd forgotten had only been buried. It had taken so little to lift it to the surface. He wanted to resist—to pull free again. Drowsily he gazed across the fields. He'd go riding as soon as it was light. He needed to feel that liberation—the complete freedom as the wind whipped and knocked the breath from his lungs, racing faster than he could ever run, jumping high enough to feel as if he were flying for the briefest of seconds. Yes. He needed that escape. He needed to ride—hard and fast and free.

CHAPTER TEN

'HESTER.'

Hester blinked drowsily. 'Mmm…?'

'Are you awake?'

Her vision focused. Alek was in the doorway, fully dressed and looking vitally handsome in slim-fit black jeans and a black shirt and gleaming black boots.

'What time is it?' She coughed the question because her insides had turned to jelly.

'Mid-morning.' He leaned against the doorframe and shot her a lazy smile.

Hester gaped—she'd slept like the dead. She didn't even *remember* coming to bed or if he'd even been in this bed *with* her. Disappointment struck. So much for thinking he might want her again or that he'd intended this to be a real honeymoon. She glanced at the table to avoid his eyes. Her box sat in the centre of it and she knew he'd put it there for her to see first thing so she wouldn't fret about it.

'I wondered if you'd like to ride with me,' he said.

'On a horse?' The question slipped out before she thought better of it and her heart hollowed out the second she realised the implication of what she'd said.

'Uh...' He looked diverted but then his smile flashed back. 'Yes. A horse.'

'Um...' She paused, prevaricating while she tried to think of...anything. Ideally a reason or excuse to say no. But her brain was failing her. She'd not wanted anything from anyone in so long and it was safest that way but now she felt heat and confusion and awkwardness and that *fear*.

'Are you afraid to try something in case you're not good at it?' He tilted sideways to take up residence against the doorframe in that gorgeous way of his.

She gave up on any pretence and just let the truth slip out. 'No. I'm afraid of everything.'

And what she was most afraid of was that what had happened between them wasn't going to happen again. When they'd talked last night she'd felt as if they'd crossed into another level—her heart had ached for what he'd been through. In opening up with him she'd thought they'd forged even more of a connection than the fireworks of their physical compatibility the night before. She'd developed faith in him and every one of her barriers had fallen. She'd relaxed so much in his company that she'd actually fallen *asleep* on him in the middle of a conversation. She'd never been that relaxed with anyone, *ever*.

'I don't believe that,' Alek challenged. 'Not for a second.'

'It's true.'

'Then you're even braver than I already believed.' He cocked his head. 'Because you do it anyway. Even terrified, you get on with what's necessary.'

She willed her brain to work so she could push back her own weakness. 'Yes, but fortunately I don't consider sitting on a massive animal as *necessary*, Alek.'

'But it's so much *fun*,' he goaded with that irresistible grin. 'Come on, Hester, it's just another little adventure and we adventure quite well together, don't you think?'

She gazed at him, sunk already. She couldn't say no to him. She'd never been able to. Not the day he'd made his convenient proposal to her. And not now. 'I'll come watch you.'

'Oh?' Triumph lit his eyes. 'See you down there in five.'

She pulled on jeans and a tee. Downstairs she picked up a pastry from the platter that was on the table and headed out to the beautiful yard. To her relief there was no one there other than Alek. She took one look at the two enormous horses saddled and tethered behind him and almost choked on her chunk of croissant.

'Uh… I'm really not sure.' She shook her head.

'Bess is very old, very gentle,' he assured her, gently patting the chestnut horse.

'And the other one?' She glanced at the jet-black gigantic creature on the other side of him.

'Is mine.'

She didn't need to look at him to know he was smiling and somehow her pride flared.

'Okay.' She drew in a breath and squared her shoulders. 'I'm fine. This'll be fine.'

'Hester,' he said softly.

She looked at him, confused by his gently warning tone.

'Don't hide again. Not with me. Not now.'

'Hide?'

'You've just assumed your calm demeanour. It's the way you keep yourself at a distance. You don't need to do that with me any more. I know the truth.'

'The truth?' Her lungs shivered. He knew how much she wanted him?

'You've already told me you're scared.'

To avoid meeting his gaze and revealing that *other* truth, Hester moved quickly. She could do this. Lots of people got on horses all the time— how hard could it be? She looked at the horse and stepped on the small stool waiting beside it. She held onto the saddle, eyed the stirrup and braced. But suddenly the horse shifted, she missed the stirrup, lost balance and in a flash had fallen. It turned out the ground was hard.

She shut her eyes, utterly mortified as she heard Alek crouch beside her. 'Are you hurt?'

'No.' But she realised she was unconsciously rubbing her rump. 'And don't even think about kissing it better.'

Embarrassment swamped her the following second. What was it with her mouth running off before her brain kicked in? He probably hadn't thought of doing *that* at all. *She* was the one fixated on the thought of kissing—and touching, and everything else.

'Only this would happen to me,' she groaned.

'I can't tell you how many times I've fallen off.' He laughed.

'I didn't even manage to get *on*, Alek.'

'Just sit there for a moment.' He turned his head. 'It's okay.' He raised his voice. 'We're okay.'

Oh, heavens, he wasn't talking to her. 'Are there people watching? They saw that? Great.'

His eyes crinkled at the corners and their coal-black centres gleamed. 'I thought you didn't care what people thought.'

'Of course I do. I mean, I try very hard not to and most of the time that works, but sometimes it doesn't and I...don't know what I'm say-

ing when you're just sitting here grinning at me.'
She rubbed her head, feeling so hot and embarrassed while wishing he were closer still and she
was still rabbiting on in a way that she never normally did. That 'calm demeanour' he reckoned
she had? Shattered. Toasted in the fiery brilliance
that was Alek himself.

'Didn't you see my scar the other night? You
know, the one on my butt?' He chuckled as the
heat spread further over her face. 'I took the most
stupid tumble off my pony onto a very pointy
stick when I was about seven. Everyone laughed
so hard.'

'Everyone?'

'My parents, the staff...' He shrugged. 'It's a
good scar. I'm sure you saw it...or do you want
me to show you now?'

'No,' she lied, then laughed, then sighed.
'You're going to make me try and get on that
horse again, aren't you?'

'I'm not sure anyone can make you do anything,' he teased.

'Don't try to make me feel competent at this
when we both know I'm not. It's all right for you,'
she muttered quietly. 'You're used to it. You know
what to do.'

'It's just practice, Hester.' He reached out to
brush her face and whispered, 'What if you ride
with me?'

She stared into his bottomless eyes. 'On Bess?'

'No, on Jupiter.' That wickedness gleamed again. 'He's named for his size.'

'Of course he is.' She rolled her eyes. 'If I can't get on Bess, how do you think I'm going to get on Gigantor?'

'Jupiter,' he corrected with another laugh. 'I'll help you.' He took her hand and tugged her to her feet.

She stood nervously as Alek shifted the small stool. His hands were firm on her waist as he hoisted her with ease, ensuring she was safely astride the animal before releasing her. She clung to the reins nervously as Alek vaulted up behind her with superhuman agility.

'You can let go now. I've got him. And you.' Alek's breath was warm in her ear and she heard his amusement as he put his arms around her. He pressed his palm against her belly and pulled her back to lean against his chest.

She drew a shaky breath in because this felt extremely intimate and precarious. They were up *high*.

'Don't worry,' he murmured. 'We'll start slow.'

She closed her eyes for an instant, transported back to that magical night when he'd turned her in his arms and made her feel impossibly good things. But then she blinked as Alek made a clicking noise with his mouth and the horse moved.

She heard his laughter as she tensed. He pulled her back against him firmly again and kept his hand pressed on her stomach. She gave up resisting and just leaned against him. He talked endlessly, telling her the names of the horses grazing in the fields as they passed them but she didn't remember a single one. His voice simply mesmerised her as he pointed out other features of the ranch as Jupiter carried them along a pathway that narrowed as they headed towards a forested area.

'These islands are volcanic,' Alek explained. 'While there's apparently no threat of an eruption any time soon, we do get some interesting geographical features.'

'Really?' She mocked his tour-guide tone. 'Such as?'

'Such as wait and see.'

She felt his laughter rumble again and her stomach somersaulted. Being held in his arms like this just made all her unrequited-lust feelings burn brighter still. It would take nothing to turn her head and press her lips to his neck. It took everything to stop herself from doing it.

Alek pressed his knees, urging Jupiter forward, faster. He wanted to get to the forest sooner. Having Hester in front of him like this was pure torture. He'd been pacing downstairs for hours waiting for her to wake up, yet not wanting to disturb her too soon because she'd obviously been exhausted. And now she was in his arms but not the way he really wanted. The battle within was long lost. He wanted her again and damn any complicated consequences. Yet he still ached. With what he'd told her? What she'd told him?

'I'm sorry we brought your cousins to Triscari,' he blurted.

'I wanted to be a princess for a day,' she said ruefully. 'I wanted to look like I had the fairy tale. Just for that moment. Just for once. Because I do still care, just a little. That's pretty stupid, right?'

'No, I think it's pretty normal.' He totally understood that she'd want to prove herself to them. 'I always wanted *not* to be a prince for a day, so I get it.'

'Does it ever happen? Do you ever get to have a day off?'

'I have one now.'

She was quiet for a while, but he felt her stiffness slowly return.

'When this ends, I want everyone to think I walked away from you. I don't want to be the victim all over again. I'd rather be seen as the evil cow who broke your heart. That it was me who chose. That I had the power.' Slight laughter shook her slim body. 'Can your ego handle that battering?'

'Absolutely.' But he felt choked. He didn't want to think about this ending yet. He didn't want to consider the moment when she'd walk out and not look back. But at the same time he wanted her to feel the power that she sought. He wanted her to know she actually had it already. She was strong and beautiful.

'They'll never believe it, of course,' she groaned. 'But I can pretend.'

'They'll believe it,' he said. 'It wouldn't surprise them to hear I've been a jerk.'

She shook her head. 'You weren't that bad. You just needed to find some fun, right? A blow-out now and then. Especially given you never get a day off.'

He didn't regret his past actions, but he didn't feel any desire to replicate them. The thought of being with anyone else now was abhorrent. Irritation needled his flesh. He didn't understand how everything had changed in such a short amount of time. He urged Jupiter to move faster, taking the excuse to hold her more tightly. Her breathing quickened, but her body moved with his. In the forest it was quiet and felt even more intimate. Through the trees he spied the blue sea and felt that familiar exhilaration and peace. 'The view is amazing, isn't it?' he said.

'Yes.'

'And then there's this.' His very favourite place in the world.

'Is that steam?' Hester asked. 'Is it a thermal pool?'

'Yeah.' He smiled; smart cookie. He guided Jupiter carefully around the large rocks and to the left of the small steaming pond.

'Can we swim in it?'

'Yes. No one else comes here. It's completely private.' It was his.

'And those rocks—they're amazing.'

'Yeah—there's volcanic glass—obsidian—in them. Sometimes I find pieces broken off.'

'It's the colour of your eyes,' she murmured. 'This is your wait-and-see moment.' She was very still against him and her voice was the thinnest whisper. 'It's like some ancient fairyland. It's just incredible, Alek. It's like…a fantasy. There's nothing more, is there? Because what with the palace and the castle and the homestead and now this?'

'This is the best place in the world, Hester.' His chest warmed as she softly babbled on, for once not holding back on expressing anything. And he was happy to confess his own secret love for it. 'I think so, anyway.'

'But am I going to have to get off this horse now?' Her voice had gone even smaller.

He chuckled, tightening his arm across her waist. 'It wasn't so unbearable, was it?'

It had been *completely* unbearable. The raw

sexuality Hester felt emanating behind her was making her steamier than the gorgeous-looking thermal pool. She hadn't been able to resist pressing back, indulging in his heat and strength, the security in his hold and the danger in the press of his thighs as he'd guided the horse to a faster pace. The wind had whipped her hair and stolen her breath before it could reach her lungs, exhilarating and liberating. She'd become appallingly aroused and he'd brought her here—to paradise. She never wanted to return to reality.

'Stay there a sec.' He swung and leapt off the horse, landing so easily all the way down there on the ground.

He turned back to face her and held his arms out to help her down. She literally slithered off the saddle and into his embrace—somehow ended up pressed against his chest. His hands ran down her back, pushing her closer against him, and she shut her eyes tightly, savouring the moment before he pulled fractionally away.

'Hester.'

She didn't answer, didn't move, didn't open her eyes.

'Look at me,' he said softly.

Neither her fight nor flight instincts were working. She'd frozen with the worst emotion of all—*longing*.

'Hester.'

She opened her eyes, lifting her chin to gaze at him, pinioned by a riot of yearning. She'd thought—so naively—that once that curiosity had been quenched, it would end. That it had mostly been only curiosity driving her to let him in. Instead, she'd discovered the utter delight of him and she wanted more. There were myriad things she secretly desired to do with him now. To do *to* him. She'd not thought she'd ever want to share any part of herself, ever. But with him?

'You know you can practise your riding skills on me any time,' he said huskily.

Oh, he was just pure temptation.

'What, as if you're some stallion who needs breaking in?' she muttered, but couldn't hide her breathlessness.

His eyebrows lifted and his eyes widened. 'Maybe. While you're the skittish filly who needs a gentle touch to bring her round.'

'Maybe I don't need that gentle of a touch.'

His smile vanished, leaving only raw intensity. 'And maybe I don't need to be controlled.'

The electricity between them crackled. The tension tore her self-control to shreds.

Why should this be difficult? Why shouldn't she reach out and take what *she* wanted? She'd been isolated and alone and denied touch for so long. And while she knew this wasn't going to last, why shouldn't she enjoy everything this arrangement with him could offer?

She couldn't deny herself. She reached for him, tilting her chin to kiss him. His arms swept back around her, pulling her right off her feet. She clung to him as every ounce of need unravelled—forcing her to ensnare him. To keep him close. She kissed him as if there were no tomorrow. But he tore his mouth free.

'I need to...uh... I need to sort Jupiter... It'll just take a moment.' He shook his head and firmly set her at a distance but she saw the tremble in his hands as he released her.

The strongest sense of liberation swept over her as she faced the thermal springs. She stripped off her tee and her trousers, sliding her underwear off too. She wanted to be *free*. She carefully stepped into the narrow pool and then sank lower, letting the silken, warm water soothe her oversensitive body.

'Hester?'

She turned at his choked sound and saw him standing at the edge of the small pond. He was still and intent.

Her awareness heightened and a deeply buried instinct kicked in. She stood, suddenly certain of her own sensuality as she stepped out of the water. She had no designer dress, no makeup. She was just plain, unadorned Hester. Completely bared. But the way he was looking at her? The response that he couldn't conceal?

He believed she was beautiful. He *wanted* her. He ached the same way she did.

Pride and power exploded within her.

For the first time in her life she was *unafraid* to take what she wanted. He could take it— more than that, she knew he willed it for her. For her to find that freedom to explore, to claim, even to conquer. It was almost anger that built within her—a reckless force so fierce and hot she couldn't contain it. That searing need drove her to take what she wanted. And that was simply to get closer to him. To seek that sensual obliteration and satisfaction from him, with him.

She unbuttoned his shirt with a dexterity she'd never imagined possessing. He said nothing but the rise and fall of his glorious chest quickened and suddenly he moved to kick off his boots. But then he was hers again. She unfastened his trousers, freeing him to her gaze, her touch, her total exploration. And she kissed him everywhere.

She pushed and he tumbled. She rose above him, savouring the sensation of having his strength between her legs. She didn't just open up and allow him in, but actively claimed what he was offering. She took, her hands sweeping over him, and she drew on the hot, slick power of him. She couldn't contain her desire any more—

it was utterly unleashed and she was hungry. *So* hungry she was angry with it. With the depth of the need she felt for him. The ache that only he filled yet that grew larger every moment she spent with him. She wanted to end it—this *craving*. The sheer ferocity of it stole her breath so for a second she stilled.

He reached up and cupped the side of her face. 'Don't stop. Do what you want.'

'I want you.'

'You already have me. Hester.'

The way he sighed her name was her undoing. She slid on him—taking him right into her soul. She heard his muttered oath, the broken growls of encouragement as he urged her on, fiercer. Faster. His sighs of pleasure scorched her, catapulting her beyond her own limits. Until she shrieked as he exploded her world.

Dazed, she collapsed on him. She'd felt nothing like this kind of physical exhaustion or satisfaction.

'Hester,' he whispered. 'Hester, Hester, Hester.' He shuddered and his arms tightened again. 'What you do to me.'

Alek sprawled on the ground, holding her close, shattered by the most elemental experience of his life. He wasn't sure his heart rate would ever recover. She was a chaotic bundle of limbs in his arms. He didn't want this fragile connection to be severed—for her to retreat behind her emotional walls again. So he slid his hand beneath her jaw, tilting her face so he could kiss her and keep her soft and pliable and warm. But she shivered. He moved, gathering her properly into his arms and rising to his knees, then feet. He carried her to the pond and carefully stepped in, holding her to him so they were both warmed and soothed by the thermal water. She floated in his arms and he teased with pushing her away only to pull her close and kiss her over and over and over until, impossible as it was, his body hardened with need again and he slid deep into her, locking her close on him, rocking them together until the pleasure poured between them and through them, brilliant and free.

A long while later he lifted her from the water. As he climbed out after her, something dug into his heel. He reached down and picked up the small chunk of obsidian. He weighed it in his palm for a moment. He could give it to her so she could put it in that box of hers and remember this even when she'd walked away from Triscari. When she left him.

He glanced at her—she looked shattered by the passion that had exploded between them. She didn't speak. Nor did he. For once he had no idea what to say—no smooth little joke or something to lighten the intensity. He'd lost all charm, all calm. It felt as if he were still standing on something sharp and the only way to ease it was by touching her.

So he dressed alongside her in silence, pocketing the stone and swiftly readying Jupiter because he needed to feel Hester resting against him again soon.

They still didn't speak as they rode back to the homestead. He knew they were going to have to address their 'contract' at some point. But that time wasn't now. Now was the time to keep holding her in his arms and pleasuring her.

But that was a fantasy too far. Instead the world was waiting for him. As soon as he saw his assistant together with his housekeeper, he knew duty had come knocking, otherwise they'd still be off-site. He cursed inwardly as Hester stiffened. Of course she understood what the welcome committee meant.

'Your Highness.' His assistant bowed stiffly while looking apologetic at the same time. 'An issue has arisen. We need to return to the palace immediately.'

CHAPTER ELEVEN

ALEK GLANCED AT his watch and grimaced. His eyes felt gritty and he could hardly concentrate on what it was his advisor was asking.

The 'issue' dragging them back after only one measly night away was nothing that couldn't have waited another day or three. It had just been palace officials stressed about his absence and using the smallest drama to summon him back. And that annoyed him. Why couldn't he spend a full day making love to his wife? But now he'd stopped to think about it, that he'd *wanted* to do that was even more of a concern.

It had been Hester who'd solved the foreign dignitaries issue—with a few quiet suggestions to him that he'd amplified to his advisors. She was intelligent and diligent and a damn good problem-solver. He'd selfishly kept her with him as he was consumed by meetings and obligations until he'd seen her losing colour and remembered how tired she'd been. So he'd sent her in the direction of her apartment and continued without her late into the evening. She'd been fast asleep when he'd returned to the apartment and he hadn't had the heart to wake her.

And now he was back there was no escape from the duties, the questions, the decisions that everyone wanted from him. He'd ended up back in conference with courtiers first thing. Which was good. Space from her would shake off that lingering concern, wouldn't it? He'd concentrate on the multitude of tasks at hand and push back that creeping sense of discomfort.

But it felt as if a craggy boulder were slowly and inexorably rolling into his gut, weighing him down further and further as every second ticked by. Those conversations he'd had with Hester at Triscari Stud had been too raw, raising elements of his past that were better off buried. Things he'd not thought of in for ever. Things that, now he'd recalled them, didn't seem inclined to return to that safe stasis easily or quickly.

He'd forgotten so much. And now he'd remembered? That stuff hurt. That stuff wouldn't be shaken. So it was good to lurch from meeting to meeting, to force every brain cell to focus on debates and decisions and stupid, tiny details that really didn't matter.

Except his brain kept returning to Hester. To those moments at the thermal springs. Her unfettered incredible response had been a searing delight. He'd wrapped around her, holding her close—not wanting her to retreat. Wanting no barrier to build between them again.

He stilled, suddenly realising there'd literally been nothing between them physically at all. He'd not used contraception. In that wild, free moment, he'd not stopped to consider *anything* other than getting closer to her. In all his years, in all his exploits, he'd never once failed to use protection. He'd never once risked it. But at the time it hadn't even occurred to him. He couldn't have cared less in his haste to have her.

Which meant he might've got her pregnant. Hester might be carrying his child.

His vision tunnelled. He'd not wanted children. Ever. Even though he knew he was going to have to at some point, he'd figured he could delay it for as long as possible. But now?

Now he had Hester. And she might be pregnant.

He felt as if parts of a puzzle had slid into place without him paying attention. But now he did. If she'd got pregnant would it really matter? Wouldn't they just stay married?

Surprising as it was, that thought didn't horrify him at all. In fact, completely weirdly, that rock weighing on his gut actually eased off. They worked well together—she was skilled and capable. There was no reason why this couldn't become a successful marriage long term. It would answer all their issues, wouldn't it?

She would have the security and safety she'd never had. The viciousness of her cousins and her school bullies appalled him and, while she seemed well free of them now, he didn't want her to suffer like that ever again. He could keep her safe with him. The media might have their moments, but they could shake that off. His life was constricted and that would impact on her—but surely it was better than what she'd had. Surely what he could offer her outweighed those negatives?

He glanced up as the door opened, half hoping Hester might've come to check on him—drawn to him in the same way he was to her. But it was his private assistant who entered.

'I apologise for the interruption, Your Highness, but you requested we update you on your wife if—'

'What's happened?' Alek's instincts sharpened.

'She's walking in the gardens, sir.' His assistant flashed a deferential but reassuring smile. 'But I don't think she realised that it's public viewing time.'

Alek frowned. 'Has she been seen by someone?'

'Her bodyguard believes they might be family members, sir.'

'Damn.' Alek strode straight to the door.

* * *

'I didn't realise you were still here.' Hester remained still, refusing to obey the urge to run away. She didn't have Alek and Fi either side of her, but she could handle the unholy cousinly trinity of Joshua, Brittany and Kimberly now, right?

'The invitation included staying for the coronation,' Joshua said with the faintest edge of belligerence. 'We're looking around the gardens.'

Hester nodded, momentarily unable to think of a reply. They reminded her of crocodiles with their toothy smiles and tough skin and she was instantly cast into freeze mode.

'You look pale,' Kimberly commented with a concern that was a touch *too* solicitous. 'Are you feeling well?'

'Very well.' Hester breathed slowly to regulate her skipping pulse. 'Thank you.'

'I imagine it's been frantic,' Kimberly added. 'Such an unexpected whirlwind wedding, Hester. How *fortunate* he found you.'

'Yes.' Brittany had been watching closely with her sharp eyes. 'You've done so well for yourself, I could hardly believe it was *you* when you walked into that chapel. What an *amazing* dress and make-up job.'

Their peals of laughter reverberated with a cruel edge and Hester all but choked. Because they knew and she knew—it was all a façade, as *fake* as their flattery and smiles were now. Smoke and mirrors.

'And now Alek can be crowned King.' Brittany sent another stabbing look towards Hester. 'But I'd have thought you'd look more like a blushingly happy bride.'

Her cousins had said nothing overtly cruel. Not even they would dare spit bare barbs and bitchiness at her in the palace grounds. No, this was a subtle poison, wrapped in layers of saccharine politeness. But they'd always known where to strike for maximum hurt—mean girls from the moment she'd met them.

Don't reply. Don't give them ammunition.

But that was the old Hester whispering. The one who'd been too afraid to speak or stand up, who'd hidden every reaction, who'd run away...

As Alek had pointed out, there was nothing wrong with choosing not to stick around to be abused. It had taken strength for her to walk out and because she had, she was even stronger now. So she wasn't going to let them chip away her new-found confidence. She'd taken on a huge job here and nailed it. What was more, while Alek mightn't love her, he liked her and he respected what she could offer.

'Oh, I'm very happy,' Hester dredged up enough serenity to assure them. 'Just a little tired from our secret honeymoon. We weren't supposed to go away, what with the coronation so soon, but—' she shrugged and her oh-so-polite tone matched theirs '—Alek's very used to doing and having what he wants.' She paused for a moment to bestow them with a smile as brilliantly fake as theirs had been. 'And he wants me.'

It was true, after all. Even if only for now.

The satisfaction she felt wasn't from seeing her cousins slack-jawed, but from the sudden lightening of her soul. What these people thought of her *truly* didn't matter and she didn't need to bother any more.

'If you'll excuse me…' She stepped past her cousins only to see her security officer standing at a slight distance behind them. Worse, *Alek* was standing beside him.

She froze. She'd been so focused on her cousins she'd not noticed him arrive. Now she saw the question in his eye and knew he'd heard some of that conversation. Her composure began to crumble.

'Is everything all right, Hester?' he asked, his gaze fixed on her.

'Perfectly fine, Alek,' she said clearly, despite her pulse pounding again in her ears. 'But Kimberly, Brittany and Joshua were just explaining that unfortunately they're unable to stay for the coronation. They need to return home tonight.'

'Oh, I see.' Alek swiftly turned to their security officer. 'Could you please escort our guests back to their hotel now and ensure they get on the next available flight this afternoon?'

'Of course, Your Highness.' The security stepped forward with an authoritative air.

Hester watched as her cousins—with furious wordlessness—walked out of her life.

'Are you okay?' Alek asked softly once they were beyond earshot.

She nodded. 'I'm fine.' She flashed a wobbly grin at him. 'I actually mean that. I handled them *fine*.'

'Not fine, Hester.' A chuckle broke his tense expression. 'You eviscerated them.'

Alek watched a raft of expressions cross Hester's face. She was much easier to read now—anger melded with satisfaction, but quickly faded to wispy sadness, to settle on bittersweet relief. It was a mash-up of conflicting emotions that made her so very human. He'd watched, frankly awed, as she'd stood her ground and despatched her former bullies. She'd breathed ice-cool fire.

Those flames within her were so well hidden, but when she let them show? She was incredible. He guided her through the gardens to the terrace and into his private study. He closed the door, determined to be alone with her again.

'I was thinking,' he muttered. 'I don't think this should end.'

'Pardon?' She shot him a confused look.

'Our marriage.' He cleared his throat and discovered how truly horrible awkwardness felt. 'You realise we had unprotected sex yesterday.'

Her skin mottled and she ducked her head, brushing the swing of her hair back with a shaking hand. 'Oh, I should have told you at the time but I... I wasn't thinking,' she mumbled. 'I won't get pregnant. I'm on contraception for other reasons. I'm sorry if you've been worried.'

'Worried? No.' He needed a moment to absorb the hit of disappointment. It was startling and he had to clear his throat again. 'Well, I think that we should tear up the contract.'

Her eyes widened. 'Tear it up?' she echoed. 'You want this to end already?'

'No. I mean stay married,' he clarified.

'Stay married.'

She seemed to be stuck on repeat.

'That's right.' He nodded. 'For good.'

She just stared at him.

'I will have to have children some day,' he said.

She didn't even blink. 'I thought you had years to figure that out.'

'I think perhaps I've figured it out already.' He watched her closely. 'I'm not going to lie. I didn't think I wanted them. Partly because I don't want to burden them with…everything. But perhaps the sooner I have children, the longer I'll be around to be King, so they can have as long as possible to shape their own lives, have their own careers, their own dreams.'

She was still staring at him, still unmoving.

'We work well together, Hester. We could make a good team.'

Why wasn't she smiling? Why was she staring at him aghast, as if he'd said something insane? Why did he feel as if he'd just tried to run through a boggy field wearing woollen socks?

'You're willing to settle for…' She trailed off. 'Just for that?'

'What do you mean "settle"?' This made sense. 'I don't think I'd be settling, Hester.'

'What about *your* dreams, Alek?'

'My what?'

'Your dreams.'

He shook his head blankly, because that wasn't the point. That wasn't ever the point.

'You don't have any?' she asked softly.

His gaze narrowed as she stepped closer. She'd done a magnificent job of masking her emotions with her hideous cousins, but her façade had truly cracked wide now. Now there was pure golden fire. 'What about *mine*?' she asked.

'Uh…um…'

'You want me to stay married to you?' she clarified. 'To have children with you? So are you saying you're in love with me?'

Hester held her breath, but for once in his life her charming, usually so smooth husband was lost for words.

'Didn't think so,' she muttered. 'You rebelled so much against the control the Crown—that tradition, your father—all exerted over you. Would you really just accept that little now? Really agree to live such an empty life?'

His gaze narrowed. 'Who's to say it would be empty?'

Had he been concerned he'd got her pregnant and decided he'd better offer to make this a permanent deal? Her heart ached because for a second there, just for a second, she'd wanted to believe he meant it for *real*.

'For so long, I've felt like I didn't fit in,' she said.

'You fit in just fine here. You know we could make this work.'

'I want more than to just make something *work*.'

And when he bored of her? What then?

'We're a lot alike, Hester,' he argued. 'You don't really want all that either. You were happy to accept a convenient marriage.'

'Temporarily, yes. But, actually, I *do* want "all that".'

She wanted the whole package—marriage and children, a family built on a foundation of love. The love she'd not had since her parents died. And the irony of it was that it was thanks to the confidence and appreciation Alek had given her that she finally recognised that she could and should.

'I deserve "all that".'

'You could have *everything* here.'

'And what's that? What's "everything"?'

'Security. Safety.'

'That's what you think I need?' She gazed at him. 'Because that's *not* everything. That's not the most important thing to me.'

'Hester, it's what you need.'

'Is that really what you think?' She gazed at him, horrified. Did he think he was 'helping' her somehow? Rescuing her? Trying to fix her life for her because he'd been unable to do that in his past? Because he'd seen her horrible cousins? 'Am I just a win for your wannabe doctor ego?' she asked, hurt. 'I don't want to be that. I don't want your pity.'

'You don't have it.' Arrogance glittered.

She didn't believe him. 'When we first met, you were furious at the fact you had to get married. You thought a marriage of convenience was the worst thing ever and you wanted to fling your own choice in their faces. But now you've decided it's everything you've ever wanted? What, something superficial, some purely contractual, cool paperwork?'

'We're hardly cool paperwork between the sheets, Hester.'

'That's just… That's not anything more than sex for you. You don't want anything actually emotional.'

His jaw hardened and a wary look entered his eyes. 'And you do?'

She looked at him sadly. 'I've not let anyone close to me in a long, long time. Do you truly think I don't feel anything more than just lust for you?'

He stilled and his expression shuttered. 'Hester—'

But she was struggling to maintain her composure. 'I don't want to settle for safety and security. I want it *all*, Alek.'

He pressed his lips together. 'What is it "all", Hester? Moonbeams and fairy tales?'

'Love isn't an impossible fairy tale to me.' She gazed at him. 'My parents loved each other. I think yours did too.'

He'd turned into a statue. But she couldn't stop her emotions from seeping through her once formidable control as in this most terrible of moments her feelings crystallised. Her ability to stay calm—to maintain her mask—vanished.

'And yes, that's the "everything", the "all" I want. Love. And, honestly, I want it with you.'

He looked winded—as if *she'd* sucker-punched *him* instead of the other way round.

'I can't...say the same to you.'

Of course he couldn't. It was the cruellest moment of her life—when she was so close, but so far from the one thing she really wanted.

'It's not you—'

'Don't.' She held up her hand.

'I can't offer that to anyone, Hester.' He overrode her furiously. 'I never have, never will. It's not in my make-up.'

'That's such a cop-out. Why? You're that afraid?'

'It's not about being afraid,' he snapped. 'I just wanted—'

'What? To make me feel better? To make me feel safe?'

He glared at her. 'And what is so wrong with that?'

'I don't need you to keep me safe. I don't need you to feel secure in my life. I just stood up to the worst people ever...and I didn't need you there to do that.'

He swallowed.

'I can do more than survive now, Alek. I can

fight for what I want. The irony is that's because of you.' She shook her head. 'You've made me feel like I can.'

He didn't love her. He wanted her, yes, but that wasn't enough.

'And what I want—what I really want—is everything, "all that" and more with *you*. But because you don't feel that deeply for me, you can't understand that you're hurting me without even realising it. That? That you couldn't see that? You might be happy to live such a superficial, safe existence, Alek, but I'm not.'

'You think I'm shallow?'

'I'd hoped you weren't. You're good to your sister. I get that you're trying to be good to me. You don't understand how heartless it really is.'

'Heartless?' He scowled and his control began to slip. 'Would you rather I lied to you?'

'Of course not.'

He was angry. 'Are you going to run away because I can't give you what you want?'

'No. I only run away from abuse, and I know you won't hurt me more now. I made a commitment to you and I won't renege on our contract. But we go back to business.'

'What does that mean?'

'I won't sleep with you any more.'

'No more kissing? No more touching? You really think that's possible?'

He looked so disbelieving it was insulting.

'It's the only way I will stay for the duration until our divorce.'

'You'll need to lock the door, Hester. But not from me.'

'I know I will. But I'll lock the door and I'll throw away the key.'

'If it's going to be that much of a challenge, then why fight it? Why not just accept that we're good together, Hester? There's no real reason why *that* can't last.'

But it wasn't enough for her. She'd told him how she really felt and he still didn't understand.

'You're really not used to not getting your own way, are you?' She gaped at him. 'Listen to me, Alek. I want more. And I'm worth more. And I will never settle for the little you're offering.'

She fled from the room, slamming the door behind her before she stared at him too long and surrendered everything regardless.

Almost all her life she'd not had it all. She'd not felt secure and cared for. She'd not felt safe enough to care for others too. He'd opened her up. She'd allowed herself to fall for someone. To love.

But she wanted to be loved in return. Loved the way other people were. She knew she'd shut down and hidden away, but she'd not realised how entrenched her defensiveness had become. She'd forgotten that she actually had things to offer people. Alek had reminded her. And made her believe she was beautiful. She could open up and share in joy and pleasure. She could engage with people beyond a quick moment in which to help someone in some superficial way. He'd made her feel warmth again—from companionship and closeness and, above all, humour. He'd changed her.

But while she'd changed him—it wasn't in the same way. The adjustment to his offer wasn't enough. And it hurt more than anything.

CHAPTER TWELVE

HESTER STARED AT her reflection, barely recognising the sleek, stylish woman in the mirror as herself. This coronation was more important than their wedding. It was the reason *for* the wedding—so Alek could fulfil the duty conferred on him from birth.

This was what he'd wanted and truthfully it was *all* he'd wanted. Their affair had been a mere cherry on his already massive cake. No doubt he'd have plenty more cherries in the future.

He might've thought they'd make a good team but it would never last. Because what he'd offered wouldn't be enough for her. She'd be hurt more and more and more knowing that she loved him in a way he would never return. When she'd had so little for so long, she couldn't do that to herself.

The teardrop diamond necklace that had been sent to her room earlier hung like an icy noose around her neck, reminding her of the heartbreak she faced. A year was an interminable amount of time. She wished he'd see that there was no need for them to wait that long. But she'd promised him she'd stay. In public, she'd hold her head high and play her part. Thankfully the palace was large enough for her to avoid him at all other times. She would run away to her apartment and survive. Eventually she'd return to the States—or maybe somewhere else entirely. Then she'd start again. She just had to get through this coronation today.

All the years of hiding her emotions were going to stand her in good stead. It was the only way she was going to get through this and do her job. Because that was her one thing—she was damn good at her job.

It was worse than if she'd run away. She was still present, still doing everything he'd initially asked, but she'd become like a will-o'-the-wisp around the palace. He heard her footsteps but never spoke to her. Caught her scent but never saw her. She was incredibly skilled at making herself invisible. Because she knew what she had to do to survive—and for her that meant not seeing him.

That hurt.

And how badly *he* wanted to see her hurt too. When he was with her, he felt good. She'd slipped under his skin and exposed old wounds to sunlight. It had hurt, tearing off those crusted wrappers. But the salve was Hester herself.

He'd not given anyone real meaning in his life in a long time because it hadn't been a risk he'd been prepared to take. He hadn't even realised how hurt he'd been. He'd not seen the truth. He'd accused her of being prickly and defensive when he was the one holding back. He'd thought he was whole and happy. But he'd been a heartless coward.

But she'd asked him what his dreams were. No one had asked him that, ever, he didn't think. And he hadn't thought he had any. Until now. *She'd* ignited new dreams, enabling him to imagine beyond merely passing personal pleasure. She'd made him realise the emptiness in his life that he'd have denied he felt only a few short weeks ago.

She'd wakened within him the possibility of a future that held more than duty. The prospect of private happiness—of laughter and fulfilment for himself. He wanted—ached—to inspire that in her. He wanted to be the one *she* dreamed about in the way he dreamed about her. He actually wanted this marriage—with her. And children—with her. He wanted to be the father he'd not had—one who was there. One who *listened*.

She made him want everything he'd deluded himself into believing he dreaded—one woman. Children. Love.

He'd been so wrong about her. He'd thought

her shy—she wasn't shy; biddable—where she was intractable, and dutiful—when she could be so defiant it made his blood sing. He'd been unable to admit how much she'd come to mean to him—not to himself. Not to her. Which mean she was right and he was a coward. It took strength to leave a situation, to speak up for what you wanted. He'd been weak in offering less than what either of them wanted or deserved. And in not opening up properly—in not allowing himself to be vulnerable the way she had—he'd hurt her. And he couldn't stand to know that.

The solution had dawned on him early this morning—after another long, sleepless, heart-searching night.

Now, as she slowly made her approach towards him in front of millions again, he realised she'd retreated further behind her walls than ever before.

Her ball gown was of epic proportions—it was the colour of the ocean surrounding the islands while the scarlet regal sash crossed her breast. This time her hair was swept up high. Long silk gloves hid, not just her fingers, but her wrists, right to her elbows. It was impenetrable armour.

But while her face was beautifully made up, he saw through to the emotion-ravaged pallor beneath. He saw the tearful torment in her eyes for that snippet of a second before she looked to the floor again. She was so formal. So correct. So dutiful. And he hated it.

He'd hurt her too badly and the knowledge gutted him. He curled his hands into fists, barely containing the self-directed anger building within him. Barely restraining his urge to run to her and haul her into his arms and beg her forgiveness.

He had to do this properly.

He didn't want her to kneel in front of him. He wanted her to stand beside him. He *needed* her beside him. She strengthened him and he hoped he could strengthen her.

For so long she'd been able to hide behind those walls. Self-contained and in control, masking her emotions, trying to bury everything so deeply so nothing and no one could hurt her. But he knew her walls were built with the thinnest of glass now and with one false move of his, they'd shatter. He didn't want to do that to her. Not here, not now. He'd hurt her too much already. He'd never seen anyone as brittle and as fragile. Or as determined.

So while he was filled with pain for hurting her, he was also consumed with pride and awe. Because she walked towards him smoothly, hidden courage lifting every step. She was loyal and considerate and frankly loving, even when he didn't deserve it.

He was determined to deserve it. And he was determined to show her how much she mattered.

Hester couldn't hold Alek's gaze. He looked so stern it scalded her heart. The last thing she wanted was to walk towards him in front of the world. This packed room was enough, but this was being broadcast again to millions over the Internet. But she had to lead the way for the rest of the citizens in his kingdom. Tradition dictated she display deference before him. Before all of them.

Her blood burned as she kept her eyes on the floor. Slowly she walked to the edge of the dais on which he stood in his cloak and crown. She couldn't look at him even then. The media would probably interpret her body language as submission and that was fine by her. Because she didn't want anyone to guess that it was pure pain and hopeless love.

Slowly she knelt before him. There was a moment of complete silence, then she heard movement as all those people behind her lowered to their knees as well.

She couldn't bear to look at him. It was all just a pretence anyway—just the part she'd promised to play. She'd grit her teeth through the final act and in a year's time she'd leave and, fingers crossed, never see him again.

'Hester.'

His soft call was a command she had to obey. Looking up, she saw he'd moved closer, right to the edge of the dais. But his solemn stare still left welts on her heart.

'I will not let you kneel before me.' His harsh whisper rasped against her flayed skin, stinging like salt rubbed across raw cuts.

She stared at him blankly.

He bent and took her hand and tugged, but she frowned and didn't move. With an impatient grunt he put his hands on her waist and physically lifted her to her feet, pressing her against him for the merest moment.

'What—?'

'Not long and we'll be alone, Hester. Trust me until then, okay?'

It was the quickest whisper in her ear so that no camera could capture the movement of his lips and no distant microphone could amplify the secret speech.

Why was he insisting she stand? Why he was going so far off-script of this massive pantomime they'd been preparing for?

Murmurs rippled across the crowd behind her. The courtiers and guests had remained kneeling, but they were looking up. Alek had stepped to the side briefly but now turned. She saw he held a crown in his hands—a smaller one than his but no less ornate.

He met her gaze for only a moment before looking beyond her to his wide-eyed citizens.

'Allow me a moment to explain,' Alek said. 'I am proud of Triscari's traditions and I will honour them but I also look forward to building new ones.' His face was ashen and his smile so faint. 'I do not wish for my most important partner to bow before me.'

Another murmur rippled across the crowd, but Alek kept talking and they silenced.

'It is a bittersweet time, this coronation, because it only happens because we have lost my father and he was a great king. He was devoted to our country and you, his people. But he was also a lonely man after my mother died. As my sister is, my mother was intelligent, progressive and loving. Losing her was very difficult for us as a family. We do not speak of her enough. I will confess, I thought the requirement for the monarch to be married was archaic—that it was a constraint and a form of control. It is only recently that I've realised it was never for the country's benefit, but for my own. To find a partner, a woman with whom I could share everything—riches and rewards, hope and dreams, and also the weight of this crown. So it is my honour, my privilege, to bow before *you*. To offer my life in service to my people, my country. And finally to offer my love to my Queen—Hester.'

Vaguely she heard cheering through the stone walls—the crowds outside were shouting his name over and over again. Not just his name. Her name too.

'Alek and Hester!'
'Alek and Hester!'
'Alek and Hester!'

Now he was staring straight at her, willing her to move. She couldn't ignore him, yet it hurt, this public display of unity that was so false. But his intense, unwavering gaze and the emotion emanating from him were all-encompassing. Surely it was something she had to reject?

But she couldn't. Not because of the crowds watching, but because of *him*. He compelled her to move with just that promise in his eyes. And even though she couldn't trust it, she couldn't deny him. So she stepped forward and took her place on the dais beside him. He turned and placed the crown on her head—the fine-wrought gold the delicate mate of his.

To her amazement, he then bowed before her. Without prompting, without even thinking about it, she dropped into a curtsey before him. They rose together and he reached out to take her hand. This was good because the air was rushing around her and she felt faint. To the beat of those chanting voices, they walked the length of the grand hall and out to the balcony. Time sped crazily as they stood in front of the gathered crowds and the clicking cameras and listened to the hum of reporters broadcasting their commentaries.

Eventually he turned and guided her back into the palace and into the nearest escape room.

'We need a few minutes.' He shut the door in the face of the palace official seeking to follow them.

Keeping her back to him, Hester stepped further into the room to gather herself.

'You...' She trailed off, realising she couldn't speak about anything too personal without losing it. 'That was an amazing spectacle,' she said harshly, indescribably angry all of a sudden. 'You really nailed it.'

His muttered oath sounded suspiciously close.

'Hester, look at me.' His hands were on her shoulders and he spun her to face him.

His eyes blazed with an emotion she couldn't hope to analyse and couldn't bear to face.

'It's wasn't a *spectacle*,' he said furiously. 'It wasn't some show for public consumption. I meant it. Every word. Not for them. For you.'

She stared up at him, stunned into rigidity.

'I don't want to do any of this without you. I was a jerk. I'm sorry. I was never more serious in my life than when I said you are my Queen. *You're* who I want by my side, always.'

She got that he thought they were a good fit.

That she could complement him. But it wasn't enough. She shook her head. 'I can't—'

'I know what I offered wasn't enough for you, Hester. I thought I understood, but I didn't. It wasn't until we were apart these last few days that I realised just how hollow my words were. How stupid.'

Her mouth dried.

'I had my walls too, Hester, I just didn't realise. All those women? It was avoidance. I didn't want to get close to anyone and never stopped to think why. You helped me—you opened me up and I realise I never dealt with any of it: the ache of losing Mother of watching Dad retreat into isolation and control. And that I'd done the exact same thing in my own way. I thought I was so clever when, actually, I'm a coward.' He huffed out a powerful sigh. 'I thought you were the one who was shut off—and you were. But you're braver than I've ever been. You realised what more you really need and you decided to fight for it.'

'That was only because you got through to me. *You* made me realise how much I was worth. And how much I really want.'

'How much you *deserve*.' His chest rose and fell. 'I know it's all been too fast but give me a chance, Hester. Give *us* time. We're amazing together.'

Amazing together? She blinked.

'Hester, I've fallen in love with you.'

She stared at him fixedly. 'That's not possible.'

'Why?' That old smile twitched. 'Haven't you fallen for me?'

She swallowed. 'Yes, but—'

'The only problem was I couldn't admit it to *myself*. I couldn't admit how much *you* mattered. I was able to keep anyone from mattering much for a very long time. But you slid into my life and suddenly everything was upside down and inside out. Me, *I'm* inside out—I'm unable to exist the way I used to. Because it isn't enough for me any more either. I want you right with me. I can't stand the thought of losing you. I hate this distance we've had.' He was shaking. 'I know it's a lot to ask. I know my life comes with a whole lot of pressure and complication. But you belong here—this could be your home. Stay with me, Hester. Please.'

'You didn't really want me to before. Not like this.'

'Because I was an idiot. Because I didn't know how to handle my own feelings. Because I was afraid. Losing someone you love hurts, Hester. I didn't realise how much I was avoiding letting myself love someone. But the fact is, I can't stop myself and I don't want to any more. I love you. And I want you to let me love you.'

She shrivelled inside. Not believing him while at the same time wanting to.

'Is it so hard to believe that I could love you?' he asked.

'It's been a long time...'

'I know.' He brushed her cheek with the backs of his fingers in the way that made her feel *precious*. 'But I think a lot of other people are going to love you, if you let them. A whole country full.'

That scared her, a lot. 'I don't want all that...' she mumbled. It felt like such pressure and all that mattered to her was him. 'I just want you.'

'And you have me.' He drew in a deep breath. 'You're so beautiful.' He leaned closer. 'You're loyal and brave and funny and kind and so very organised.'

She almost smiled.

'But if you don't want to stay here, we can work something out.' He glanced at her. 'I don't quite know——' He broke off.

'Of course I want to stay, Alek.' Of course she would stand beside him, do anything she could to help him. Just as she was beginning to realise that he would for her. 'I want to be with you. To work with you.'

His hands swept to her waist to hold her still, but it was the look in his eyes that transfixed her. She didn't notice their finery; the gold and jewels faded into insignificance because all that mattered was the emotion shining so clearly in his eyes.

'I have something for you.' He unfastened the top two buttons of his jacket and reached into the inside breast pocket. He pulled his fist out and unfurled his fingers in front of her. A small shard of obsidian sat in his palm. 'It's from that afternoon at the springs.'

'You took a piece?'

'At the time I thought...'

'Thought what?'

'That you might put it with that button in your box.' He gazed into her eyes, his own a little shy. 'But *I* wanted the reminder, that's why I didn't give it to you then. And now I know we should collect more memories *together*.'

Little treasures from little moments that meant so much more than any precious jewels ever could.

He put the obsidian in her palm and locked his hand around hers. What he'd given her was beyond precious—it was access to his heart, his soul. And she would always keep it safe. Just as he was offering to keep her heart safe in his hand too.

He was here for her. He wanted her. He loved her.

Her eyes filled as he swept her into his arms. But he kissed the tears away. He pressed her close against him as if he were afraid she'd disappear if he didn't; his grip was almost painful. But she revelled in it—rising to meet his mouth with hers. To pour every ounce of soaring emotion back into him. She loved him. And he loved her.

'I should've known when I realised I wasn't terrified by the thought of you being pregnant,' he confessed with a breathy laugh. 'I never thought I wanted kids, now I can't wait. I want to see you cradling our babies. I want to see a whole bunch of miniature Hesters curled up in a big chair and reading their favourite books.'

She laughed through her tears. 'While mini Aleks will wow everyone with their ventriloquism?'

'Something like that.' He pulled her close again. 'You believe me?'

She rested her head against his chest and wrapped her arms around his waist, needing to feel him against her and know he was solid and real. 'I will.'

'I know, we need some time together alone.' He sighed. 'But right now we have to go in there for a while. Can you handle it?' He sounded apologetic.

She lifted her face to smile up at him. They'd have their time alone together soon enough and she couldn't wait for that magic. But she understood that right now Alek had the obligations of that heavy crown upon him. It was a burden she'd gladly help him shoulder.

His answering smile reflected the joy rippling through her veins. She rose up on tiptoe to kiss him and whisper her absolute truth.

'I can handle anything when I have you beside me.'

EPILOGUE

Two years later

'COME RIDE WITH ME.'

Hester glanced up and registered the heat of intent in her husband's eyes. 'I thought you had meetings all afternoon?' she asked, faking cool serenity. But she put down the book she'd been reading and quickly stood.

'Finished early.' Alek smiled knowingly.

She knew that smile so well and every time he sent it her way, it hit her right in the solar plexus. He didn't just love her, he *adored* her—making her feel beautiful inside and out. And with him at her side, she didn't just handle everything— all the good and the bad—that life had to offer, she *revelled* in it.

So now she drank in the sight of him in the black trousers and shirt he preferred to ride in. Sensual attraction fluttered as she felt ruthless desire emanating from him. Their need for touch hadn't dissipated in the two years since their mad, quick and convenient marriage—in fact it had increased.

After the coronation they'd had to escape—stealing a full month of a real honeymoon at the stud, replying to any arising issues via phone and emails. And even then, upon their return, it had been a challenge to concentrate for longer periods of work again.

Together they'd formed their alliance. She'd accompanied him more on engagements and she'd found a purpose of her own in reinvigorating the city's literacy programmes. Then, just this year, she'd opened the children's library of her dreams—using a room in Queen Aleksandrina's castle, to bring life and love and laughter back to the place, so that more people could take time out there and appreciate the beauty built by an untameable woman who'd refused to fit in.

And every weekend they could, they came back here to Triscari Stud to oversee the breeding programme and take some time for themselves. So now Hester walked with him to the yard. Jupiter was saddled and waiting not quite patiently. They always rode together when staying at the stud even though Hester had learned to ride on her own and actually found she wasn't just getting better, she enjoyed it.

Today Jupiter carried them both. Alek steered him in the direction of the clifftop forest that they'd gone to on her first visit here. Hester's heart sang as, sure enough, they went to the hot springs where they'd come together again in that desperately passionate way. She treasured that piece of obsidian that rested safely in her box. But today it wasn't only the striking rock formations and steaming water that caught her attention. A circular white tent was set up near the pool and a small sofa actually sat outside in the warm sun, smothered in plump cushions and rugs.

'What's this?'

'Our anniversary escape.' He tightened his hold on her. 'Or did you think I'd forgotten?'

'I didn't think you'd forgotten,' she murmured. 'I thought you were probably planning something for later. I figured your meeting was a cover.'

'Were you planning something?'

She smiled coyly and leaned back against him. 'Of course.'

She loved dreaming up nice things to show she cared. Small things, to treat him, and he did the same for her—slowly building their own language of care and love and collecting the trinkets to put in their shared memory box. But this time she had the most perfect secret to surprise him with.

She slipped down from Jupiter and walked towards the tent. Fairy lights were wound around the wooden poles while the interior was filled with fresh flowers and a pile of soft-looking wool throws artfully strewn on a bed. There was a small table with a wicker basket beside it that she knew would be filled with their favourite picnic food.

'Going for comfort this time?' she teased him.

'Going to stay the whole night.' He nodded. 'Maybe even two nights.'

She curled her toes with delight. There was nothing better than stealing time for just the two of them. She'd never known such fulfilment and happiness.

'So...' He leaned back to look into her eyes. 'Has my bringing you here caused any problem for what you had planned?'

She shook her head. 'My plan was vague but portable.' Her heart pounded and to her amazement tears formed, bathing her eyeballs in hot acid that spilled before she could speak any more.

Alek's eyes widened. 'Hester?'

She nodded quickly. 'I'm fine.' All the emotion clogged her throat so she could only whisper. 'I'm better than fine. You know...'

He still frowned but a small smile curved his mouth and his hold on her tightened. The contact strengthened her. She trusted him completely—knew she could expose herself, reveal her greatest vulnerability—because he always caught her. He always listened. He cared.

'I'm pregnant,' she blurted.

He stared, frozen for eternity before his expression exploded with intensity. 'Say it again.'

'We're having a baby.'

Because this was *them*, together, and their little unit of two was going to become three.

A huge rush of air hissed from his lungs and she felt the impact as relief and joy and incredulity radiated from him.

'It's been hideous keeping it from you these last couple of days.' She lifted her hands to frame his beloved face. 'But I wanted to save it just long enough to tell you today.' She rose on tiptoe and pressed her tear-stained mouth to his.

They'd decided to delay trying for a little while after their wedding so they could discover and delight in each other and solidify the intense connection they'd forged so quickly. But a few months ago they'd discarded any contraception. And now? Now her joy was so fierce, it burgeoned, encompassing him too.

'Not going to lie—I'm terrified. But I can't wait, Hester.'

He pressed her to him and she felt his strong muscles shaking.

'We can still make love? Is it safe—?'

'There'll only be danger if we don't!' She laughed and growled at the same time. 'I need to have my way with you, my King.'

'Well, you are my Queen and I will always bow before you.' He didn't just bow, he dropped to his knees, his hands firm on her hips as he gazed up the length of her still-slim body. 'I can't wait to meet our child, Hester.'

'Neither can I.' She dropped to her knees too— desperate to feel again the pleasure that was only theirs.

With him she was free and utterly unafraid to reveal everything—her body, her soul, her secrets—all the things that scared her, all the things that delighted her. He didn't just accept them, he embraced them, and he shared his own so together they were stronger still.

'Alek…' she breathed, enraptured by the fantasy world into which he'd cast her.

'I'm here, Hester.'

And he was.

Because beneath it all—the crowns, the diamonds, the palaces and castles…everything— their love was real.

* * * * *